THE
DREAM LOOM

Christie Monson

Park Place Publications

THE DREAM LOOM

Christie Monson

Copyright © 2020 Christie Monson

ISBN 978-1-953120-05-2

First Edition September 2020

Park Place Publications
Pacific Grove, California
parkplacepublications.com

Cover images by Shutterstock
Cover design by Maria Morales-Solorio

to my husband, Tim Calvert,
with all my love
in this world and the next

The world is full of magic things,
patiently waiting for our senses to grow sharper.

W. B. Yeats

Part One

May

Thursday morning

The three women sat together on the edge of the bed. The floral print curtains were closed, filtering the morning light.

"She's worried, Mahina."

The large bronze-skinned woman nodded and continued to watch. "Yes, Betty, she is."

"She doesn't know if it's real, or just nerves."

Mahina nodded again. "Rebecca will be fine. But, depending on what she decides, her life could change radically."

"I just wish …." Betty began with a tremor in her voice. She shrugged and shook her head. "I wish that I'd been able to be of more help to her before this happened. If only things could have been healed first, well, she might feel better equipped."

The third woman spoke up. "You've done everything you could. Sometimes these things have to unfold in their own time, dear."

Betty considered this for a moment. "I suppose so. Thanks, Lydia." She looked at the slender woman with her white hair in a bun, and smiled her appreciation.

Rebecca clambered up from the bathroom floor. Leaning heavily against the tile counter, she brushed her teeth, rinsing well. She shuffled into the bedroom. Oblivious to the presence of the three women, she sat, dazed, in the corner armchair.

Eventually, she stood and rummaged through her closet to get ready for work.

Mahina gathered her long wavy hair, dark brown with streaks of white, and let it fall behind her. She raised her palms skyward. "My friends, we are on the brink of a new adventure!"

Lydia laughed. "We are, indeed," she said. She rubbed Betty's shoulders to reassure her.

"Will she really be all right, Mahina?" Betty asked.

Mahina watched Rebecca a little longer. "Yes, she will. And if she makes the decision I expect her to, the person she will soon meet could be a tremendous help to us all."

The three women watched her for another moment, then nodded at each other. An opalescent shimmer surrounded them, and they vanished.

Rebecca continued to dress in silence.

*   *   *

Thursday afternoon

Rebecca found the aisle quickly enough, though she'd never needed to buy one of these things before. She felt like someone else—at least, not like herself—as she stood in the checkout line. Usually the clerks barely noticed her as they scanned her items; she was just one more in a continuous line of boring customers. But this time, after the routine scripted greeting and bagging the purchase, the clerk flicked her head up to look fully at Rebecca's face. Maybe she took a second glance at anyone buying a pregnancy test. Or maybe it was because Rebecca had smile lines and traces of gray in her hair.

Rebecca dropped the toilet lid and sat. Staring at the plus mark on the test strip pinched between her thumb and forefinger, she clutched her brown French braid in her other hand as if it were the only thing that anchored her to the planet. She pictured telling Reuben. This was not something they had entertained even remotely. Images of holding a baby swirled in her mind and felt incomprehensible, foreign. She closed her eyes and breathed slowly in and out as she tried to calm her mind.

The faint scent of her sandalwood shower gel brought her back to the room. She stared at the outdated, cracked terracotta tile with the ugly yellow fleur-de-lis. Since buying this house, she had wanted to tear it out and replace it with fresher colors. At this moment, it seemed important to memorize the space, the sea-foam green towels hanging there, the mangled toothpaste tube with its cap off, and her hair blower with the cord now in a permanent series of twists. Her eyes returned to the test strip. She stood abruptly and flung it into the trash.

At the sink, she stared into the mirror. Could she have imagined, the last time she had consciously looked at herself, that she would ever need to contend with a pregnancy? She searched her face and whispered, "What in the *hell* am I going to do?"

She couldn't call Reuben yet. He had a staff meeting after school today. Besides, she wanted first to get a better grasp on all this herself. At this point, she didn't know what she wanted. She wouldn't know what to say.

She changed out of her teaching clothes into shorts, T-shirt, and grubby shoes. Red plaid curtains swung wildly against the dark wooden back door as she slammed it behind her. She needed to get to her garden; digging in the dirt always made her calmer and helped to clear her head.

The scent of jasmine wafted to her, compelling her to pause for a moment and take in her surroundings. Overgrown stone paths meandered through the little yard that she—contrary to nursery guidelines about spacing—had filled with all of her favorite plants close together when she moved in three years ago. Already, flowers crowded and tangled in a joyful chaos of color that contrasted with the drab San Francisco Bay overcast on the warm May afternoon.

The entire yard was enclosed by a six-foot-high wooden fence covered with orange trumpet vine, white jasmine, and purple potato vine, and she savored the privacy it afforded her. (There were, however, two loose planks that the neighbor's cat could squeeze through for visits.) The plum tree in the center of the yard already had tiny green plums on it. By July she would be out here, face to the sun, sucking the fruit's sweet juicy red flesh from its tart dark skin—her private indulgence.

Satsuma plum. *Prunus salicina*. Botanical names always gave her solace. There was something solid and ancient about

Latin: unchangeable, secure, regardless of the present moment. It helped her to shift into a more stable reality. She found it comforting, especially now.

"*Acanthus mollis,*" she greeted the bear's breech, which had begun to bloom. She loved how the white and purple flowers opened sequentially up the long spikes. So far, only the lowermost blooms were open. She bent down and brushed the edges of one bloom gently with her fingers. How soothing to know what was going to happen next. No surprises.

No surprises.

She heaved a sigh and consciously made her way along the stone path, careful not to step on any plants. Maybe it wasn't true. She couldn't really be pregnant. She'd had sex all these years without one scare. How could this be happening? Maybe it was a false positive. She could get another test and check it again.

The woodsy-spicy scent of dried leaves mixed with the crushed green aromas of ground foliage. Determined to restore calm, she greeted aloud, "*Viola odorata,*" sweet violets in their fragrant purple, with yellow freckled centers and heart-shaped leaves, almost finished for the season, snuggled next to the rock cress, with its clumps of deep pink, round-petaled flowers, now at their peak. Ozark sundrops, with their bright lemony trumpets burst forth from a forest of narrow, pale green leaves.

She stepped carefully among the peach-toned daylilies to reach the garden shed. It was partly hidden by the large spiky leaves of *Filipendula rubra*—Queen of the Prairie, whose bits of feathery rose-pink blooms sprinkled over Rebecca's head as she lifted the branches and propped them onto the roof so that she could open the door. *"Filipendula rubra,"* she said, moving her lips consciously around each syllable. The wooden shed was weather-bleached and splintery, but the latch slid aside easily enough to allow the door to creak open. She selected gloves, a large bucket, and a low stool. (She used to sit cross-legged on the ground to pull weeds, but now her knees complained at that angle.) The air was cooler in the shed's interior, quiet … earthy smelling … peaceful. She brushed dried soil and cobwebs from her stack of terracotta pots. One pot held a variety of bulbs she'd meant to plant last fall. She picked up one tulip bulb. *"Tulipa gesneriana,"* she chanted. Holding it in her hand, she ran her thumb over the dry, light-brown lump, reflecting that such a small unobtrusive thing could transform into a green plant with large blooms. Like an unborn baby, she thought, and her heart thudded with the reminder.

Shaken, she picked up her supplies and trudged to the middle of the garden. She settled the foot-high stool into the dirt and sat. Slipping on her gloves, she dug gently around the red and white geraniums (*Pelargonium x hortorum:* "the *stork* of gardens," a translation she couldn't prevent herself from recalling), pulling a dandelion out of the loose, moist soil, slowly, so slowly that she could feel the hairy tips of the roots letting go with a series of quiet pops. A clump of grass, slowly, slowly, easing out, pop, pop, fffff, ahhh. No fighting, just a quiet giving up. One weed, one clump of grass at a time, into the bucket.

But what if it was true? She massaged her forehead, smudging it with dirt. Could she give birth at this point in her life without endangering her health? Wouldn't it be even more difficult because she'd never had a baby before? She rested her head in her hands, trying to come up with a coherent thought, when something bumped her elbow, startling her.

A small tabby cat rubbed against her leg with a loud purr.

"Nutmeg, you little scamp!" She scratched the cat behind his ears and he nestled his head against her gloved hand. Nutmeg was petite for a full-grown cat. He had spent many afternoons with Rebecca while she worked in her yard. She was glad for his company now. "I've done it this time, buddy. I don't know what to do." The cat's eyes closed to contented slits as he reveled under her caresses, apparently unconcerned about anything beyond this moment.

"I sure wish I knew how to relax the way you do." He hopped onto her lap and settled in. Rebecca petted him absentmindedly. "Animals' lives sure are simple. You get pregnant—or in your case, you get your girlfriend pregnant—and you don't stop to worry about what the future holds. An animal mother doesn't worry if her body can handle it. She just does it."

Rebecca watched him purring, eyes closed. "Oh, sure. You've been fixed, haven't you? Reuben and I both had always meant to do that. Now look at the mess we're in."

The cat twisted onto his back and looked at the garden from his upside-down position.

How was Reuben going to react to this? He was always there for his boys, but would he be up for raising another baby? Could she do this alone? Would she be okay? Would a baby born at this stage in her life even be okay? She stopped petting the cat. He righted himself and insisted his head against her hand. "Oh, Nutmeg!" She stroked his neck slowly and whispered, "What am I going to do?"

From the corner of her eye, a glint of light caught Rebecca's attention. *What was that?* She turned and scanned the garden, but didn't see anything unusual. The flicker of light—if it had been there at all—was gone now. Maybe it was just stress.

But Nutmeg had noticed something, too. With a cheerful purr, he jumped from Rebecca's lap. He tiptoed across the yard, his tail twitching, toward the spot that Rebecca had been eyeing. Well, maybe some little critter had scrambled up the fence.

She took off her gloves. She hated the futile job of trying to dig the dirt out from under her fingernails, but she couldn't resist the feel of the earth, of communing with something timeless and nurturing. She took off her shoes and socks, shuffled her feet back and forth in the dry dirt until they found the cool underlayer of earth greeting her tender soles, filling the space under her arches. She dug her fingers into the black dirt, rubbed it between her palms, and held her hands to her face, inhaling the mineral dampness. She dropped her hands and gazed across the yard, seeing it, but not seeing it.

She could get an abortion. No. That went against everything she'd ever believed. But she was forty-nine. Maybe that made it different; maybe she had to let go of her old ideals. But would it haunt her afterward if she did? And after all of her forceful expressions of her view about this to others, wouldn't this make her a flagrant hypocrite? Would she admit to anyone she had done it? Or would she keep it a secret? How would that feel to her, long after the fact? Now, she admitted with a feeling of deflation, she understood more about the struggles of other women in this situation.

She turned to her Christmas rose, its pale pink blossoms almost done for the year, and immersed herself in pulling every last weed she could find, refusing to let her brain get involved. Focus. Ease out the roots, shake off the dirt, throw into the bucket. Find another; repeat. She watched a ladybug meander up the outside of a rose petal and delicately reposition itself at the edge before beginning its descent into the center of the rose.

She arched her back to relieve it from too much bending forward, then scanned for more weeds. There were none left within reach, and she didn't feel like getting up to move again. Her bucket was nearly full.

Hands still on the small of her back, her thoughts quickened again. Even if the birth went okay, even if the baby were healthy, she couldn't raise a kid! Just occasionally babysitting Kate's girls exhausted her. And she valued her solitude so much. If she did this, she sure wouldn't get any of that anymore. And this baby would have old parents. Kids get so embarrassed about that. Maybe she should go through the birth but give it up for adoption. Even if Reuben was up for this ....

Her throat tightened. She longed for Reuben to be here now, holding her, helping her to believe that she could handle this after all. She found strength in the smallest things with him, like how they could make each other laugh, or the way he took her hand when they talked. She loved playing with his wavy dark hair, now mixed with a bit of gray. His beard, also starting to show some gray, had grown out a bit lately, which—she had noticed the other night—made it softer. And the soap he used left a subtle spice scent on his skin that made her feel safe and nurtured.

She thought of him with his boys, the last time they'd all had dinner together. Jeffrey and Ben, now grown, often got together with him, all talking easily with each other. Reuben had shared all of the parenting responsibilities with his ex-wife while the boys were growing up. Rebecca couldn't ask for a better partner in parenting. But he was fifty-two, and he'd already worked so hard raising Jeffrey and Ben. Would he be willing to do it all over again? He always talked about wanting to travel.

She felt angry at the baby. *Don't show up now, of all times, for God's sake! You've got to go. No. No! This is impossible! It's got to go.* She loosened the soil around her roses and re-dug the water wells next to them, deeper than necessary. *No. Dammit. When I was younger, I could have done this. But not now!*

A breeze came up, bringing her the jasmine's perfume from across the yard. She closed her eyes in gratitude for the distraction and gathered strength from the earth supporting her bare feet. She thought of Reuben, of how well they understood each other, how her heart had opened with him more than in any other relationship she'd ever experienced.

When she opened her eyes, the leaves of the plum tree were still waving in the breeze. Something caught her eye, and she saw another sparkle of light, this time just above the rosebush beside her. She looked for Nutmeg to see if he was reacting to it, but the cat was across the yard with his back to her, batting at a jasmine tendril. She turned back to the rosebush and scrutinized it. Nothing unusual now.

She shook her head and stared into space. She was probably just tired and her eyes weren't focusing properly. She moved to the next section of the garden. Gently holding the bellflower stalks aside, she slid her other hand in, pulled out three dandelions, and tossed them into the bucket. She stopped. She pictured going into the abortion clinic. She pictured leaving afterward.

Reflexively, she put both garden-encrusted hands on her belly—not as flat and firm as it used to be, and, of course, no outward sign of a baby yet. Still …. Now she could imagine a life within her. A real person. Someone she could get to know!

And then … she imagined that person *vanishing*.

She felt an abrupt surge of confused panic. Her muscles felt suddenly awake, her mind alert and protective of this child she didn't even know. *Damn!* How could she already feel connected? "This is nuts!" she said aloud.

Hands on her belly, feet flat on the ground, Rebecca sat up straight and addressed the cat, who had turned at the sound of her voice. "I'm calling Reuben right now."

*   *   *

Reuben gathered his biology students' research papers and crammed them into his briefcase. The day had been swamped with students' crises, deadlines, and administrative snafus. He scratched his beard with both hands in frustration, then closed the briefcase with an exasperated sigh. He locked his classroom door and headed down the corridor, nearly colliding with Mark at the corner.

With his tan corduroy jacket askew, Mark held his empty coffee mug and keys in one hand while he tried to tame his own pile of loosely stacked papers in the other. "Reuben," Mark said. "I was just coming to find you. You want to grab a beer?"

"I could use one." Reuben blew out a blast of air. "I'm still ticked about the meeting."

Mark put his mug and keys on the ground and restacked his papers. "It's not that what's getting added is bad, we just don't have time to do what's already required. And now they're cutting staff?" He thrust out his hand with the papers. "Where in the hell are we going to find time to give students meaningful feedback?" With a growl, he jammed the stack under his arm and retrieved his mug and keys.

Reuben grunted in agreement. "Let's get out of here. Maybe an order of Azucena's nachos with those beers will give us some inspiration."

They headed for the parking lot. The students were gone, but the lot still held many teachers' cars. As the two men wove through the cars toward the far side of the lot, Reuben's phone rang. "Hang on," he said, while Mark continued to his car. "It's Rebecca."

*   *   *

Rebecca had it all planned. She would ask Reuben to come over because she had something important to talk about. When he got there, she'd sit him down and tell him. They would discuss the whole thing like rational adults.

Reuben clicked on his phone. "Hey," he said in his familiar way.

The warmth in his voice flooded her with a wave of relief and safety. "I'm pregnant!" she blurted. She froze. *Oh, hell! What did I just do?*

She heard an eternity of silence before a confused, "What?"

"Oh! Damn! I wasn't going to say that! I was going to tell you in person! I don't know what I'm doing. Can you come over right away?"

"Uh …." Reuben stammered. "Uh, *yeah*, but …." He lowered his voice a bit—maybe for privacy, Rebecca thought. "But … tell me again?"

"I'm pregnant. Seriously."

"Uh." Reuben hesitated. "Okay, um … okay. Since you've told me anyway, tell me more before I get there. What happened? Uh, did you take a test? Did you see a doctor?"

"I've been missing my period for a while, and I just thought, well, maybe it's menopause. *This* never occurred to me until I started feeling nauseated in the mornings. At first, I told myself I was just hungry. But then this morning, I threw up. It scared me, so I went and bought a test."

Reuben was quiet.

"Are you there?" Rebecca couldn't keep the shriek out of her voice.

"Yes! Sorry! I'm just taking this in. You're sure?"

Rebecca felt herself shaking. "Talk to me. Tell me it's going to be okay. I'm really frustrated not seeing your face. I know this is hard. I know you've already done this. I can't believe this is happening. Reuben, I'm forty-nine!"

"It's okay. It's okay. It's fine. I'm fine. We'll figure it all out. I'll be right there. Do you need me to pick up anything?"

Rebecca, still shaking, realized how long it had been since lunch. "I'm starving."

"I'll get something good and be there as soon as I can."

*   *   *

Reuben pulled out of the high school parking lot. The sun was beginning to set over the Bay. Waves of peach and pink mixed with blue and burst upward into the thick high clouds that had lingered all day.

"Shit!" he said as he shifted into third. "Shit!" He raked his fingers through his hair, making it more unruly than usual. *She's pregnant? Rebecca is pregnant? No!* They were careful every time! Okay, maybe not *every* time. But they thought they were past that possibility. "Damn!" Reuben hit the steering wheel with the heel of his hand. "Dammit!"

He slowed to a stop at the light. His mind raced. He tried to concentrate. She had told Reuben that she'd never wanted to have kids, even when she was younger. Would she get an abortion? No, even with her reluctance toward parenthood, he doubted it. He thought of the debate she'd gotten into with their friends one night over drinks. "How can people who are against abortion support war? How can people who are against war support abortion? It's *all* killing. Where is the logic?" she had persisted. Reuben smiled, thinking of her passionate views. But his smile faded quickly. Rebecca was forty-nine. Wouldn't that make a difference to her? She was strong—at least in ordinary ways—but at this age, could she give birth and be all right? What if ....

Two cars honked emphatically at Reuben. He realized he'd drifted out of his lane, and quickly swerved back.

Hell. He was fifty-two. He couldn't take this on now. He already raised his boys. He was younger then, and it had been hard enough. Twenty-five years ago with Ben. Jeez! Twenty-seven with Jeffrey! That was like another lifetime! Could he rally enough motivation, enough energy to do all that again? And could Rebecca be up for this? Shit. She must be scared to death.

Rebecca. He softened and tried to slow his thoughts. Well, if he had to raise another child, he couldn't think of anyone he'd rather do it with. They understood each other. They respected each other's needs. This was clear during their recent discussions about moving in together. He felt a new wave of love for her and thought about how great she was with kids. Even the tough kids at the alternative high school, where she taught, liked her. He never got tired of watching her teach at science camp. She knew every kid, each with their own quirks, and treated them with warmth, humor, and respect. They rose to the challenge of living up to her belief in them. She'd be a great mom. He'd always thought that. Now he just might have the opportunity to see that he was right. Reuben clutched the steering wheel as this new complication asserted itself more strongly within him.

He stopped at a red light and looked around. He'd missed the turn to the café.

With dinner in bags, Reuben couldn't reach his key, so he tapped Rebecca's door with his toe. She opened it almost immediately. He paused, having no idea what to say first. Then he lifted the bags. "Struck gold," he said. "Café Ina had the beef stew you like. Biscuits, too." He headed for the kitchen.

"I can't believe I want to eat," she said. "This is all so surreal. But I'm hungry anyway."

Reuben eased the bags onto the counter. He turned to Rebecca and wrapped his arms around her, taking a big breath, trying to slow his racing mind. She clung to him and they exhaled together.

"Thanks for getting here so quickly," she said into his shoulder. "What were you doing when I called?"

He stroked her hair and kissed it. "Mark and I were just ranting about the staff meeting. We can do that any time. I told him I had to go. Didn't tell him why. He'll live."

She tightened her arms around him. "I keep thinking this is a dream. Or a nightmare."

"So …." He put his hands on her shoulders, moving back to look into her face. "Um, do you want to talk first? Or should we eat?"

She let go of him with decisive focus. "I need to eat." She strode across the kitchen and pulled bowls out of the cupboard, gathered silverware and napkins. Reuben opened packages, and they headed for the table.

They ate in silence for a while. Reuben watched Rebecca scooping stew into her mouth as if she were starving. She always did have a good appetite. But this seemed more like stress. Was she waiting for him to start the conversation? Did she want conclusions or questions? He took a breath to say something, then stopped. Maybe she just wanted quiet for a bit longer. Maybe she wanted more time to think. Or maybe she just wanted to get to the bottom of her stew. Normally, they had a great rhythm with each other, knowing when the other wanted quiet. Now he felt out of sync. He wanted to fix this thing but didn't know where to begin.

Rebecca broke into his thoughts. "This tastes good. Thanks for picking it up."

Reuben set down his fork. "So. Hmm. I have a pile of questions, and I don't know which to ask first. But bottom line, whatever you want to do, I'll back you up." Rebecca searched his eyes. He took her hand and continued, "We created this situation together; we are in it together. Whether it's short term or long term, I'm here with you. I love you. Are you clear about that?"

She slid back her chair. He did the same. They stood and met in the middle, standing, hugging, rocking. She loosened her hug and rubbed his back. He took her hands in his, kissed one open palm and then the other. "Let's go sit on the couch," he said.

They sat and stared into space, acclimating to the news together. Then she turned to him and her words tumbled out. "I can't get an abortion. I have to admit, today I actually considered it, but I just can't. I know being pregnant at my age is a terrible risk. I need to find out what that even means, but I just can't have an abortion."

He nodded and touched his hand to her cheek. "I suspected as much. It's okay. I meant what I said before. Whatever you want, I'm with you."

"Thank you." She sank into his shoulder. "I guess I knew that, but it still helps to hear. I just feel so stupid! I mean, sheesh!" She sat up again. "You and I both teach sex ed, for Pete's sake! We know how this works!" She grabbed a pillow and kneaded it. "I keep replaying over and over, the last time we … we weren't *careful*, you know?" She hugged the pillow and sat back against the couch. "And in my mind, I keep rewriting the script that we used protection instead, and wishing I really *could* re-write it. You know that writhing panic that rises in your gut, that futile drive to go back and do things differently. So you picture it again. And again. If only, if only, if *only*." She flung the pillow aside.

Reuben drew her to him. "I know," he said. I've been doing the same thing. But, we're here now. So."

Silence settled around them.

"So," he repeated. "Look at it like this. Look how good we are together. I've never known anyone like you. We can do this. We're going to be fine."

Rebecca didn't say anything.

He loosened his arms and turned to her. "We're going to be fine," he said again.

She nodded slowly. "Yeah. I think we are." She took his hand and stroked first one side, then the other.

After a while, she said, "I realized this afternoon that rather than guessing on my own, I want a real doctor to talk to. I called Ann's clinic after I called you and managed to get through to her. I know that might sound obsessive, but, honestly, I guess I'm hoping that she can tell me this is all a big misunderstanding. I want *her* to test me. I trust her more than some mass-produced kit. Even if she uses the same kind I used, I want *Ann* to do it. She's my last hope!"

He nodded. "Sounds like a good idea to talk with her."

"Yes, and she's completely booked for the next two weeks, but she could tell how upset I was and said she would come in to see me at her clinic day after tomorrow."

"On a Saturday? Whoa!"

"She's a good friend."

"I *guess.*"

"Could you come with me? I have a lot of questions, and you might have different ones. I'm not so sure my brain will be able to take in everything I need to know. Ten o'clock?"

"You've got it."

Rebecca settled beside him.

If they had a doctor's appointment, then this was real.

*   *   *

Friday

The large bronze-skinned woman closed her eyes to the sun and sighed with pleasure as the breeze fluttered her wavy hair. High above the Urubamba River, the morning mists had dissipated.

"Ahh, Churi," she said as she stroked the brown and white llama that rested on its haunches next to her. "Another beautiful moment."

The llama gave a vibrato hum in agreement.

They turned at the sound of someone climbing the rocky steps behind them. A tall bearded man came into view at the top.

"Thaddeus! Come join us."

Thaddeus paused to roll up the sleeves of his plaid shirt. "What a great hike!" he exclaimed. And this view! I can't believe I waited this long to come here."

Mahina grinned at him. "You've wanted to since you studied South America in sixth grade."

"Indeed I have," Thaddeus replied. "And I'm glad I chose today. Sprinting up these grassy slopes in this fresh mountain air is just what I need while I think about my grandson."

"Reuben is certainly feeling distressed." Mahina nodded sympathetically for a moment before adding, "But, of course, it's not as bad as he thinks."

"Mm. I wish I could convey that to him. He's been wanting to travel, too, and I think he's feeling that the dream is unreachable now."

"Did he ever talk about coming here?"

"No, I don't think Machu Picchu is on his mind." Thaddeus looked across the valley at the other tall peaks, then fifteen hundred feet down to the river. "Though he'd be crazy about this place if he saw it in person." Thaddeus sat on the ground and leaned against a granite wall, its stones fitted meticulously together. He scratched the llama behind her ears. Churi tilted her head and grunted. "Reuben's more of an ocean enthusiast. He wants to try scuba diving, that sort of thing."

"Hm." Mahina nodded. "Well, he'll get to do it all, eventually. But he doesn't know that, so it's no comfort to him right now."

"Maybe Eli has an idea."

Mahina gave him a broad smile. "That's just what I was thinking. Let's go have a chat with Eli. I know exactly where he is."

Churi watched as her two friends disappeared into a luminescent glimmer of mist. She clambered to her feet and scaled the slope to join the rest of the herd.

*　　　　　*　　　　　*

Saturday 10:00 a.m.

Rebecca and Reuben held hands as they walked down the hall to Ann's clinic. The hallway was dim and quiet with other offices closed for the weekend. Rebecca and her niece, Kate, had met Ann a couple of years ago when they joined a yoga class that Ann also attended. Rebecca appreciated Ann's kind demeanor and interest in learning new things. Rebecca had never been impressed with the doctor she was going to at the time, so she had switched to Ann.

Ann let them into the empty waiting room and locked the door behind them. Instead of her usual professional attire, she wore a denim shirt with khaki slacks and white tennis shoes.

"Thanks so much for coming in on your day off, Ann," Rebecca said.

"Oh, I have a ton of paperwork to catch up on anyway." Ann turned to Reuben. "Okay, Reuben, you get to relax while Rebecca does the test one more time and we do a quick exam. I'll let you know when we're ready for you. No one will see if you play with the blocks over there."

Reuben smiled as Ann and Rebecca disappeared down the hall. He sat and paged distractedly through a few magazines, then looked around the room. After considering for a moment, he walked over to the pile of large multicolored blocks and shifted a few around for a while. This didn't feel as fun as he'd hoped. He returned to his chair and drummed his fingers against his thighs.

After what felt like both too long and too short a time, Ann opened the door and invited him in. He followed her down the hall to her office, furnished in gentle earth tones. Ann gestured him to a two-person sofa. "Rebecca's getting dressed," she said. "She'll be here in a minute." She pulled two books from her shelf and dug through a collection of brochures.

Reuben watched Ann for a moment, then said with new resignation, "Um …. I don't suppose you give brochures to people who *aren't* pregnant?"

Ann's eyes met his and she started to reply when Rebecca walked in and sat next to Reuben. Ann pulled up a chair to make a triangle with them.

"Okay, first of all, to get you up to speed, Reuben, yes, Rebecca is pregnant."

Reuben nodded and took Rebecca's hand. It felt a little shaky.

Ann continued. "It's extremely unusual at forty-nine, and to cut to the chase, it *is* possible to have a healthy baby. But, as you know, there *are* more risks to both Rebecca and the baby.

Rebecca turned to Reuben. "The reality of this hit me more than ever when Ann and I were talking in the other room. And I told her about the research we did online last night. Risks to the baby: Down's syndrome, placenta problems, stillbirth. And I know we saw a bunch of others I can't remember now." She shook her head. "I can't believe I'm dealing with this."

Reuben directed his concerns at Ann. "Yes, and what about for Rebecca? Um ...." He hesitated before forging on. "Diabetes, hypertension?" A harshness crept into his voice. "I mean, we can talk about *odds*, but all I'm worried about is the bottom line." He stopped and tried to compose himself.

Ann nodded. "Of course. There *is* a greater risk of everything you've both mentioned. But that doesn't mean any of it will *necessarily* happen. It is true that the risks of pregnancy at this stage of life are different than for younger women. However, the plus side is that you two have the advantage of being more mature emotionally. That will be a tremendous help.

"Right now, we're guessing that you could be as much as ten weeks along. I want to do an ultrasound to be more accurate about that. And later, you can have a screening for Down syndrome and other problems, if you choose. One thing to consider, though, when deciding how much testing you want to do is, what will the results mean to you? For instance, Reuben, Rebecca has already told me that she—our favorite peacenik—is unwilling to get an abortion and that you know this."

"Yes, I do."

"Now Rebecca, these are your personal decisions to make, and it is probable that the baby will be fine. And you are starting out in good shape, so your odds of staying healthy are better than for many pregnant mothers your age. Even so, there are serious risks, and I'm sorry I can't promise what will happen."

They nodded.

Ann looked intently at Rebecca. "Above all, I want you to pay attention to what your body can handle as the pregnancy progresses, and call me if you want to discuss any doubts, or if you need a sounding board." Ann leaned forward. "This, my self-sufficient friend, is *not* the time to be a martyr."

Tears of relief rose in Reuben's eyes. "Thank you," he whispered.

Rebecca flicked her head around to look straight at him. "I thought you understood what I was saying last night."

"I do. And I agree. But," his voice cracked, "I also don't want anything to happen to *you*." He swiped at his eyes.

At the sight of Reuben's emotion, Rebecca's throat caught with her own feelings, and she touched her hand to his face. But after a moment, she recovered her resolve. "I know you're worried," she said evenly. "I'll be all right. I'm going to do this."

He hugged her hard and held on.

Ann quietly stepped out and returned with a pitcher of water and some paper cups. "Let's have some water," she said. "I can't have you dehydrating." She pulled a small side table over, poured the water, and handed them each a cup. "Okay. If you want to see this through, then you need to do a couple of things for me so that I'll be able to sleep." She pointedly made eye contact with each of them. "You don't want me to lose sleep. It makes me very cranky," she said with a dry smile. "So listen up.

"One: I'm giving you plenty of written resources to satisfy that insatiable brain of yours. But no more researching online. Sure, there's some helpful stuff out there, but there are a lot of serious inaccuracies too, a lot of scary stories. You don't need the stress. The baby doesn't need the stress. If you start wondering about something, you are allowed to use the Internet to email me. Ask *me*. Are we clear? If I get wind of you reading scary stories online, I'm going to come over to your house with my pruning shears and cut your modem connection myself."

Rebecca laughed. "Okay, okay."

Reuben smiled, but Ann said, "And this applies to you, too, Reuben."

Reuben dropped his smile and nodded. "Okay. Me, too."

"Two: You need a support system. Sure, you two are great together, but you need more. You need your village. I recommend this for anyone about to have a baby. And this applies to you at least as much as anyone else. From what I have seen, Rebecca, you seem to put a lot of stock in being ultra independent. But you need people, not just to get you through the pregnancy and birth; you will need them as you raise this child. You've told me that you have a sister and a brother, but you hardly ever see them. Would they rally around you under these circumstances?"

"Well, my real support system here in town, besides Reuben, is Ellen. We've been best friends since preschool. I know I can count on her. And my niece, Kate, and I are close, as you know from yoga class. But that's about it, when it comes to family. My parents are gone. My brother, Brad, is great, but he lives in Vermont. My sister, Martha, lives here in Berkeley, but, no. She wouldn't be supportive at all. It's really better for me to stay away from her—if you want me to avoid stress, that is."

Ann rested her elbow on the arm of her chair. "So, what's the deal with Martha?"

Rebecca proceeded to drain her cup of water in a long, slow guzzle. Reuben watched her, scooted forward on the sofa, and began.

"Rebecca and I actually met almost thirty years ago. We were married to other people then. We were all in a citywide coed soccer league. Rebecca's sister, Martha, and Martha's husband, Greg, were on the team too. The six of us socialized a lot after games. But Rebecca's marriage to Ted and my marriage to Cathy, well, they were not good."

"Huh. They were miserable," Rebecca put in. She put her cup down. "But it was not the kind of group where people were really aware of what was going on with each other. It was all about barbecuing after games and talking about the next game. That's when my sister, Martha, and Reuben's wife, Cathy, got to be close friends."

"So Cathy and I barely knew Rebecca and Ted in those

days." Reuben settled back in the couch, and Rebecca continued.

"A few years later, Ted and I divorced, and Reuben and Cathy divorced. We didn't discuss it with each other at all. We had no idea about any details until just three years ago when Reuben and I ran into each other at a science teachers' conference in Portland and got to talking."

"Over a lot of dinners and missed seminars," he added, smiling at Rebecca. She gave him a wink.

"And we discovered that we'd both had the same problem in our marriages," Rebecca continued. "Our spouses had been affectionate and romantic before we married, then afterward, almost immediately, they became workaholics—Cathy with her software company and Ted with his accounting firm. They were both so serious all the time, never wanting to do anything that wasn't work related, and there was certainly no passion. It quickly became a lonely existence, and we both started thinking—"

"Not knowing about each other's situation at the time," Reuben put in.

"—that life was too short," Rebecca said.

"After our divorces, Cathy vented to Martha, and Ted leaned on Greg, and from then on, Martha has viewed us both as evil incarnate." Reuben shrugged.

"Hm." Ann poured more water all around. "So, both divorces were how long ago?"

"Well, more than twenty years," Rebecca said. "At the time, I tried to explain it to Martha, but she sided with my ex, Ted. She clearly thinks that people should stay married no matter what." Rebecca brushed invisible dust off the seat of the couch. "Anyway, then, after a few more years of socializing with Martha and Greg, Cathy and Ted started dating, and now—get this—they're married to each other."

Ann still held the water pitcher. "You've got to be kidding me."

Reuben shook his head. "No one could make up this stuff."

"It makes sense, when you think about it," Rebecca said. "I mean, they were already friends, and no doubt they cried on each other's shoulders. And they are equally, um, *reserved*, so we figure that they are more suited to each other than we ever were with them."

"Wow. Quite a journey for all of you." Ann finally set the pitcher back on the table and sat back. "How about your family, Reuben?"

"My mom died a few years ago, but my dad is nearby. He's terrific and he'll be supportive, especially now that he's retired. I think he'll be happy to jump in and help. My sister lives in Chicago and my brother is in Austin. The three of us get along well, but we don't see each other very often. They'll both offer moral support from a distance, but it won't be all that tangible."

"How about your boys?"

"My boys. I haven't told them about this yet." Reuben opened his eyes wide and laughed. "*That'll* be interesting. But I think after they get over the surprise, they'll be fine. They like Becca a lot."

"Okay," Ann said. "We've covered enough for one day. Let's stop here. Call me if you need to. Meanwhile, both of you get plenty of rest and exercise, and *keep breathing*."

*　　　　　*　　　　　*

Saturday Noon

Brutus, an eighty-pound black Lab, bounded to Rebecca's car and shouldered her door the rest of the way open. He pounced his muddy paws onto her lap and repeatedly dragged his wide tongue across her face. His slobbery pink and black lips smelled like wet grass; indeed, there were a few green flecks stuck to them, probably now on hers as well. Rebecca, relieved that at least his lips didn't smell like anything other than grass, rubbed his tank of a torso vigorously in return greeting.

Ellen rushed out her front door and attempted to call off Brutus. Failing that, she snagged his collar and peeled him away. Her auburn hair was held in a bun with chopsticks, but several strands had come loose.

"Sorry, Becca! I guess he's missed you!"

Rebecca laughed and wiped her face on her sleeve. "It's all right," she said as she climbed out of the car. "As a matter of fact, it's *nice* to get a simple doggy greeting after all that's been going on."

"I've got chicken salad for lunch," Ellen said. "How does that sound?" She and Rebecca headed toward the house with Brutus dancing and snorting alongside. "Wait a minute, mister." Ellen guided the dog over to the hose to wash off his paws. An old towel hung on a hook by the faucet for such occasions.

"Chicken salad sounds great." Rebecca stepped into the familiarity of Ellen's house. She flung her purse onto the couch and headed for the kitchen. She loved the wide-armed welcome of the beige and teal kitchen, family room, and dining room, all in one open space. Curtainless French windows allowed plenty of light onto the woodwork and furniture.

She filled the teakettle, turned on the burner, and headed for the tea cupboard. She had plenty of time to rummage for her favorite tea before Ellen and Brutus caught up to her. Ellen's dark green sweatshirt and faded jeans had a few splashes of water on them. At her insistence, the dog loped to his bed in the dining room corner, circled over it twice, and then dropped, though he continued to watch the women with his chin on his paws.

"Thanks for making lunch," Rebecca said. "I'm starving and exhausted. Turns out, major life changes take a ton of energy. Who would have guessed?" She finished unwrapping her teabag then turned to Ellen. She realized how much tension had been in her shoulders and finally let them drop.

Ellen stepped forward with open arms and wordlessly held her in a tight embrace. Rebecca held onto her lifelong friend until the teakettle whistled.

"Okay." Ellen faced Rebecca across the table. Now that Rebecca was getting fed, Ellen could push her for details. "Tell me everything the doctor said."

Rebecca finished her mouthful. "Ann's great. She's

committed to giving me as much information as I need and working as a team with me, so I trust her. But she says I need to stop searching the Net if I want to keep my sanity. And I think she's right."

"Why?"

Rebecca stabbed her fork into a chunk of apple. "Last night I looked up what the risks were for women in their almost-fifties having babies. One site called me an 'elderly primipara.'" She pointed her full fork in the air. "*Primipara* means someone having a baby for the first time, though it reminds me of vegetables over pasta or something. And *elderly*, in this case, means someone over the age of *thirty-five* who's having a baby. Shit." Her eyes watered. "I was already depressed. And now I find they've got a name for me that makes me feel like a freak. So there we were in the exam room, Reuben was waiting down the hall, and Ann couldn't even get started because I was crying about *that*, of all things."

"Oh, honey."

"Which is so dumb! I mean, isn't it more important to talk about the actual risks? I couldn't get past the name calling." She put the apple chunk in her mouth and chewed angrily, her eyes threatening more tears.

"Becca, cut yourself some slack, for God's sake."

"Huh. You sound like Ann."

"Well?"

"I know, I know. So, *finally* I did get past the name calling, but then just talking in person with Ann made all of the possibilities feel more real."

"So now you're pretty scared."

Rebecca nodded.

Brutus heaved himself out of his bed, lumbered over to Rebecca, and planted his chin in her lap. She rubbed his ears and looked into his brown eyes that never left her.

"The thing is …." Rebecca stopped.

"What is it, hon?"

It dawned on Rebecca for the first time that she didn't want to worry Ellen. She had been about to let all of the horrible possibilities spill out, to seek comfort from her best friend. But now, to say them out loud again after already naming the risks with Ann, it was suddenly too much. She focused more intently on massaging Brutus's ears and gazed into his loyal face. Now she felt her tears build.

Ellen had abandoned her salad. "Are you thinking about what all of the risks are?"

Rebecca nodded and began to cry quietly.

Leaning on her elbows, Ellen looked thoughtfully at Rebecca for a moment. "Honey, I know how you feel about abortion." She reached for Rebecca's free hand and squeezed it. "But in this case, in these circumstances, have you considered it at all?"

Rebecca looked at her friend through blurry eyes, relieved that Ellen already knew what was troubling her. She gave Brutus a parting rub and turned back to Ellen, describing her struggles of the past few days. When she finished, both women sat quietly, letting their thoughts catch up and settle while they poked at their salads.

Ellen broke the silence. "Where's Reuben right now?"

"He and Mark are taking a long bike ride in Tilden Park.

Ellen, he's been wonderful. I couldn't ask for more support from him. I know he's scared, but he's doing this thing. He's in this with me. I'm glad he's got Mark so he can blow off steam with him. He seriously needs that." Rebecca shifted her attention to her lunch, feeling her emotions regain some balance. She picked a walnut out of her salad and ate it.

"So, what are you and Reuben going to do? Are you going to get married?"

"We've actually been talking for several months about moving in together. We've waited this long because we both really love our solitude. We have lots of stuff at each other's houses already, and our time together has become more important lately, even before the pregnancy. But marriage? We've never seen a need to consider it."

"Yes, that is you."

"It is. I'm just so afraid of ending up in a marriage like my parents had. Even though Reuben is nothing like my dad, and I'm nothing like my mom, so it's kind of irrational. I guess I can't help it."

"Welcome to the human race."

"Mm," Rebecca grimaced. "But on top of that, the past couple of days I've realized more vividly why I've avoided having kids all these years. I'm afraid I won't be able to do any better than my parents did. My family was so screwed up. I don't know what I would have done without your friendship."

"Well, it was tough putting up with you." Ellen rolled her eyes. She stood and rounded the table to give Rebecca a hug and a kiss on the cheek. "You can be a real pain." She gave her another kiss.

Rebecca sighed heavily.

Ellen hugged her again. "Becca, come on. You deserved better. You have more insight and compassion than they ever had." She put her hands on Rebecca's shoulders. "You're going to be a great mom."

Rebecca sighed a longer, slower sigh and hugged her friend with gratitude before releasing her.

Ellen returned to her chair and brushed away more strands of hair that had come loose from her bun. "Does Martha know yet?"

"Huh. No, Martha is definitely not a person I want to deal with in the middle of this. Isn't it ironic? Reuben wants to do all of this with me—classes, raising the baby, everything. He's in this all the way. Martha has condemned him for years for being irresponsible, and *she's* the one I can't rely on to be supportive."

Rebecca went to the sink and refilled her water glass. She leaned against the counter, gripping the edge as she stared out the window for a moment. "But Ann has a point about us needing to gather our village."

She returned to her seat. "Hell, I'm getting old. I mean, for being a new mom. And what if I really can't keep up? Even though Ann says I'm in great health, it's obvious this will put a strain on my body more than it would for women in their twenties. Jeesh, those little twerps can bounce back from anything."

"Tell me about it. Let's have some chocolate." Ellen got up and rummaged in her freezer. "Fudge brownie ice cream," she announced, grabbing two spoons.

"Perfect."

With the carton in the middle of the table, they both dove in.

Rebecca savored the first two creamy bites with her eyes closed. Then she examined her spoon before continuing. "The thing is, I do want a backup plan. I *am* scared. What if I don't survive the birth? If something happens to me, I need to know that someone else would help Reuben raise the baby."

"And that would be …?"

"Well, first I thought of you …."

"Ack!" Ellen shrieked. "I was afraid you were going to say that!"

Both women laughed.

"I know, I know!" Rebecca held up both hands in reassurance. "I mean, you'd be *great*!

But you're in the same boat as me, in terms of age and energy. And I think, even if I stay healthy, and I *can* keep up, kids need young adults in their lives too. To feel, you know, *normal*."

"Mm." Ellen nodded. "That is important."

"So I'm thinking Kate and Mike."

Ellen blew out a whistle. "And that brings Martha right into the mix."

"Exactly. That's my dilemma. Kate and Mike are incredible parents to Naomi and Fiona; I would love to think that they would be, I don't know, godparents?"

Ellen nodded. "And you know I'm happy to be a back-up babysitter and offer you other support you might need. But you have a point about a younger family needing to be an integral part of your network."

"Thanks." Rebecca sighed in gratitude. "But," she frowned. "I do worry. What kind of tension will it create? I mean, between Martha and Kate, and how will that affect Kate's girls, as well as my baby? Is it worth the price of that kind of tension? Maybe I should find someone else and avoid all that stress for everyone."

"Kate and Mike are the logical choice, though."

"They are. I'm going to go with that plan for now, at least. I would sleep better if I had something in place so I can worry a bit less. I'm going to bring this up with Reuben. He needs the village as much as I do, even though he hasn't acknowledged that yet. I'll see Kate at our yoga class on Tuesday night, and she and I always have dinner afterwards. I'll tell her then that I'm pregnant—sheesh! Every time I hear that out loud, I wonder who just said that—and suggest that the four of us get together soon. I know all this is early. And I *could* miscarry for all I know. But I have to make plans. I'll go nuts if don't do anything."

"All that makes sense. I'd do the same thing. I just keep thinking about what a fit Martha is going to have when she finds out about all this."

"Well, that's her problem." Rebecca turned to Brutus, who had stayed by her side, and petted his head. "Right honey?"

"You know it makes me crazy that she treats her own sister so rudely. Especially because she was like that with you even before your divorce." Ellen's voice carried an edge to it now. "Even when we were in high school, she treated you like nothing you did was good enough. It's not you *or* your divorce. It's *her.*"

"You want to hear a funny thing? Kate says that Martha is well loved in her neighborhood. Turns out that she used to take dinners over to her old neighbor, Jewel. She babysits when young parents need a night out, too. Seems she'll do anything for her neighbors. And her daughter and grandchildren."

Ellen rolled her eyes. "Well *that* makes up for how she treats *you*."

"Well, I've never stopped wondering if she'll ever lighten up, but at least I've let go of the need to try to change things. It only took me years of intensive therapy to get to that point. I'm especially glad I learned to let go before *this* came up. I'm fine now. I'm good."

Ellen opened her mouth to say something, but instead pressed her lips together. She looked directly at Rebecca and let out a loud exasperated sigh through her nose.

"Okay. I'm lying," Rebecca said softly.

"I know you are."

"It hurts like hell."

Saturday evening

A fire crackled in Rebecca's stone fireplace. Heavy fog had rolled in as the sun set, making it especially appealing to be inside. Rebecca and Reuben sat on the couch, their feet in socks on the pine coffee table. She closed her eyes and soaked in the toasty feeling on her feet and the warmth of Reuben on her left side. She cradled her mug of tea in her hands, watching the flames dance randomly with logs, accompanied by occasional soft pops. Rebecca basked in the lull for a few more minutes before breaking the quiet.

"How was your bike ride with Mark?"

"Excellent. We ripped all over the hills. It felt great. Then we locked up our bikes at Inspiration Point and hiked the trails, talked about everything." He crooked his head toward Rebecca. "So. If you were at Ellen's, then we've both talked all day about this. But is there anything else we need to talk about tonight? I have to admit, I'd love to *stop* talking for a while. But it feels weird to ignore it."

"No, I'm fried. There are a million things we'll need to consider, but I'm all talked out for now. About the heavy stuff, anyway. How about you?"

"Mark squeezed everything out of me, too. Brain and heart."

"He's a good friend."

"That he is." Reuben put his hand on her arm. "Oh. There is just one thing I wanted to tell you about before we stop. I know you've been feeling bad about my urge to retire soon and travel."

Rebecca nodded. She looked into his eyes with concern.

"I had a bizarre dream last night. My grandfather was in it, and it felt so real I can't stop thinking about it."

"Your grandfather who died when you were in college?"

"Yeah. My mom's dad. We were always close, even when I was a little kid. He was often at our house, but besides that, we hung out together a lot, just the two of us. We could talk about anything. Considering that, I guess I'm not surprised I'd think of him when all this life-changing stuff is happening."

"He sounds great. I wish I could have met him."

"You would have liked him. He was a lot of fun." Reuben paused. "Anyway, in this dream, we were sitting by a campfire in a redwood forest. We used to camp together pretty often. In the dream, the mood was so relaxed. He sits back in his camp chair and says to me, 'I know you want to travel, and now you're worried you won't get to. But trust me, Reuben, you'll still be able to do all the traveling you want. There is plenty of time, and all is well.' That's it. Then I woke up. It was pretty incredible how it felt more real than any other dream I've had. It was like he was right here."

"Wow."

Reuben took the teapot from the coffee table and lifted it toward her. "You want more?" She shook her head. He poured himself more tea and sat back.

"You know I don't put a lot of stock in dreams and all that stuff," he said, shrugging. "That's always seemed kind of 'out there' to me. And I didn't want to bring it up this morning when we were getting ready to see Ann. I mean, I still worry about your health with all this, and I seriously needed to bring up those questions with her today. But the thing is, about the reality of parenting instead of retiring? I'm just not worried about that anymore. I feel like it's enough to just be in the moment and not worry about how to fit everything in. It'll be okay. It'll all work out. Weird, huh?"

"Not too weird," Rebecca mused. "Isn't it amazing how a dream can affect your mood?"

"I guess so. Oh, there was one more thing, though it sounds pretty bizarre." He started to laugh.

She tilted her head and waited.

"There was this llama in the dream. Why is a *llama* in a redwood forest?"

She laughed. "Well, dreams can have some pretty strange elements in them. What was the llama doing?"

Reuben thought. "I'm not sure. I wasn't overly aware of it during the dream. I just woke up with some idea of a llama being there." Reuben shook his head. "I must be going nuts. Now I'm having llama dreams."

She chuckled. "No, life is strange, and so are dreams, that's all."

They leaned back and gazed at the fire. They watched the logs reduce to embers before heading for bed. As they ambled down the hall, Rebecca said, "I'm going to tell Kate after yoga on Tuesday. What about you? You getting together with the boys anytime soon?"

"I thought I'd call them tomorrow and set something up."

"It's so weird to say it out loud. I'm pregnant. Weird."

"I'm trying to picture Jeffrey and Ben when I say it. Hell, I'm just trying to picture *saying* it to them."

"Any predictions about how they'll react?"

"Well, Jeffrey's always good with the poker face. We'll see if it holds up this time. Ben? He'll probably start with 'Dude!'"

Rebecca laughed.

Sunday

The light coming through her curtains told Rebecca it was already late morning. She heard dishes clinking and smelled coffee, but she wasn't ready to get up. Her bed felt remarkably luxurious this morning. She required more time under her comforter.

She closed her eyes again. Yesterday's conversation with Ann about how she and Reuben got together replayed in her mind, and now more memories arose.

When she met Reuben for the first time on the soccer field, he had a long, dark brown ponytail and a scruffy beard. (Nice legs, too.) The team that she and Ted were on was better than Reuben and Cathy's team. But she noticed that no matter how much Reuben's team got smeared, he always had a good sense of humor about it. Not like Martha and Greg, who took every loss as a personal affront. And Reuben's wife, Cathy, acted painfully serious in every game, whether she was winning or losing. Ted was the same way. For them, games never seemed fun so much as something they should do for their health— like taking vitamins. That seemed to be how they viewed their marriages, too—like an obligation, something to do by rote.

After her divorce, Rebecca discovered that she loved being single, living alone, gathering with friends when she wanted to, dating when she wanted to, having peace and quiet when she wanted it. No headaches, no hassles. But her sister and parents never understood this. They constantly tried to "bring her around" so that she would follow the traditional script of marriage and motherhood. When she got the offer to teach in Yonah River, in the Northern California redwoods, she jumped at the chance to get away.

It was twenty years later when she ran into Reuben at the conference in Portland. They hadn't seen each other since they'd both been married to their exes. His ponytail was gone, and for the first time, she could see that he had a natural wave to his hair. His beard was starting to show a bit of gray. Rebecca thought he looked nice.

Years ago, she hadn't felt any special attraction to Reuben. But as they discovered over many meals how much they had in common, she found herself less interested in the seminars that normally enticed her, and she brightened every time she saw him.

Rebecca remembered well the lovely feeling that came over her in their earliest conversations. Here was someone who was not just supportive, but who could genuinely *understand* what her marriage had really been like and how it felt to be unfairly judged by others. Rebecca had felt something shift in her heart, as if a bulky knot that she'd never realized had been there was, at last, untying. When she told Reuben this, he knew exactly what she meant. He said that he felt like he'd finally gotten a decades-long-overdue oil and filter change. She laughed, thanked him for being so romantic, and their friendship found its true beginning.

Rebecca was smiling at this memory, nestled under the covers with her eyes closed to the morning light, when she heard a creaking floorboard in her hallway. She opened one eye.

Reuben tiptoed in. "You want some breakfast?"

Suddenly she needed to throw up.

Tuesday

The waitress—in bleached blonde pigtails and false eyelashes with royal blue glitter, wearing black tights and a mini-dress with red bandanas sewn at random angles—led Kate and her aunt, Rebecca, weaving through the rustic wooden tables to a dim corner booth. For Kate, Tuesday nights were an extra treat because Mike stayed home with their girls, making her a free woman for a few hours. She could finish sentences, eat her meal without having to help anyone else eat theirs, and go home without yogurt and spaghetti sauce smeared into her clothes. Yoga class afforded little time to chat, so the two women built in their catch-up time by having dinner afterward in downtown Berkeley. Café Gratitude was their most frequent choice. They loved the quirkiness of the bustling restaurant and that each vegan dish was named in the form of an affirmation. Each table had its own carafe of water, a small vase with flowers, and a box of cards with discussion questions on them, including, "What are you grateful for?" Surrounding them on the brick walls were multicolored paintings of planet Earth, of people holding hands around the world, and of blooming flowers larger than the people. Tonight, about half of the tables were occupied.

Handing them their menus, the waitress said with an airy lilt, "Hi, my name is Morel, and I'll be your server tonight."

"Morel?" Kate asked.

"Yes," Morel purred. "Like the mushroom."

The women smiled. "Any specials tonight, Morel?" Kate asked.

"Oh, yes! Our appetizer of the day is 'I am Insightful,'

which is spring rolls with straw mushrooms and barley sprouts. Our soup of the day is 'I am Amazing,' which has raw coconut, curry, and seaweed. Our lasagna of the day is 'I am Fabulous,' which has raw organic zucchini, tomatoes, and spinach. Can I get you a drink to start?" Morel fluttered her glittered eyelashes, creating the effect of strobe lights dancing around her nose.

"Just water." Rebecca gestured toward the carafe on the table. "And I think we know what we want. Are you ready, Kate?"

"Yep. 'I am Fortified,'" Kate affirmed.

"Would you like quinoa with that, or brown rice?"

"Quinoa. Oh, and some tahini sauce too, please. And a glass of cabernet."

"And 'I am Fabulous.'" Rebecca closed her menu and handed it to Morel.

"Perrrfect." Morel undulated away on her errand.

Kate poured water for both of them from the carafe on the table. "No wine tonight?" she asked.

Rebecca waited for Kate to make eye contact before she said, "I wanted to order 'I am Pregnant,' but they don't have that on the menu."

"Ha ha!" Kate put the carafe down, then stared at Rebecca. "Wait. What?"

Rebecca looked steadily at Kate.

"Rebecca? What? Are you serious?"

"I really am. I'm pregnant. I know, it's crazy. It's not possible. But it is." She pressed her palms to her cheeks.

Kate put her hands on her own cheeks. "I can't believe this!" She scrutinized Rebecca's face. "Are you okay?"

"Well, *stunned* would be a good word."

Kate jumped out of her chair, her long ponytail swinging, and gave Rebecca a big hug. Still holding Rebecca's shoulders, she leaned back to look into her face. "Ah. Uh …. um …. Ack!" she stuttered. "Really?" She watched her aunt nod. "Wow!" she hugged Rebecca again before sitting back down. "How is Reuben reacting?"

"He's been great. Shocked, too, of course, but he's completely supportive. We've already talked a lot and we went to see Ann a few days ago."

"So, what does she say about how you …?"

"You mean, can I do this at forty-nine? She says yes, but I have to take really good care of myself. I'm not young and fit like you are," she said, gesturing toward Kate's lean body, still in her stretchy yoga top with a skirt thrown over it. "You still look great in everything, even after giving birth twice and chasing a four-year-old and a two-year-old around all day, and you never seem to run out of energy."

"Well, I don't know about that." Kate waved off the compliment. "So, are you … you're going to do it?"

"Yep." Rebecca picked up her cloth napkin and began to fold it into a triangle, then another one, and another.

"Wow!" Kate shook her head. "I can't believe this."

"I know. I can't either. But yesterday I had to run out of my first-period class to barf, so I guess it's real." She shrugged.

"Ugh. I can sympathize with that. But, better you than me, I say." She flashed a smile at her aunt.

Rebecca swatted Kate's shoulder affectionately with her napkin. "Thanks."

"Anytime."

"So, we'd like to get together for dinner with you and Mike pretty soon."

"Sure. Can I tell …."

Morel arrived with Kate's wine and bowl of steamed vegetables with quinoa. "You are Fortified," she said with a flourish. She placed the lasagna in front of Rebecca. "And You are Fab-u-lous. Would either of you ladies like anything else?"

"Maybe we should reserve our desserts," Kate said. "What's your cheesecake of the day?"

"Ohh!" Morel rolled her eyes in ecstasy. "'I am Cherished.' Today it's chai cheesecake made with cashew cream and an almond-date crust. We also have 'I am Magnificent,' chocolate mousse made with raw cacao and almond milk."

"I am Cherished!" Kate almost shouted.

"Two of those," laughed Rebecca.

"Fan-tas-tic." Morel left.

Kate asked, "So can I go ahead and tell Mike?"

Rebecca scooped zucchini with cashew cheese onto her fork. "Yes, I think it would be good for him to have a chance to digest the news before we arrive. Reuben and I always love getting together with you all, but now we feel especially strongly about spending time with family. You know, the village thing."

"That works for us! We'd love to see more of you. The girls would, too."

The Next Week

After two chapters of *The Magic Treehouse* for Naomi, several repetitions of *Goodnight Moon* for Fiona, and many repeated choruses each of "Waltzing with Bears" and "Great Big Stars," the little girls were finally asleep. Reuben and Rebecca inched stealthily off either side of the double bed where the girls sprawled next to each other, every muscle fully relaxed. They tiptoed down the squeaky hallway, trying not to undo their work, and released triumphant whispered *ahhhs* as they stepped into the living room. Finding Mike and Kate in front of a newly built fire talking softly over glasses of cabernet, Rebecca and Reuben collapsed into the blue and yellow couch across from them.

"Hey, thanks, you two," Mike said. "We actually got to have a real conversation without interruption *or* falling asleep in the middle of it." He grinned at the two of them stretched out on the couch. "Looks like you guys need to train for this job. Feel free to practice with our girls anytime."

"Yes," Kate added. "I can see that the four of us are going to make a great team." She raised her empty glass to them before getting up to make tea.

"I love reading to your girls. Let's make it a regular thing," Rebecca said. She patted Reuben's thigh. "And Reuben started adding bear voices mid-verse. A talent I never knew he had."

Reuben rolled his eyes and shrugged. "You guys feed me good dinners like that, I'm happy to sing in my bear voice."

Mike chuckled.

"So, Mike, what's going on at work these days?" Reuben asked. "Kate says you've been working long hours."

"Yeah," Mike rubbed the back of his neck with a calloused hand. "I've already been working with a skeleton crew to keep costs down, but now one of my carpenters is in rehab, so I'm scrambling to cover for him and stay on schedule. Makes my hours brutal these days."

"Oh, man, what a pain," Reuben said.

Kate brought out the teapot and mugs. "Rose petal tea," she said. "Good for peace of spirit." She set the pot and mugs on the coffee table and they helped themselves.

Rebecca un-slouched herself and propped a few pillows behind her before picking up her mug. "So, on the topic of working as a team, I want to talk about ... well ... actually, a bit more than that."

"Sure," Mike said. "What's up?"

"Well," Rebecca began, "this might sound dramatic, but with this baby coming, I feel like it's important to be practical."

"Funny how having kids jolts you into Practical," Mike said.

"It does," Rebecca said. "And for me, because of my age, I'm especially thinking about how I'm going to handle the pregnancy." She glanced at Reuben, who looked more serious now. She touched his arm. "Reuben hates talking about this, but we agreed that we have to bring it up."

Reuben nodded.

"We don't have to talk about the obvious risks," she said. "The main thing is that we'd like to create some team parenting with you."

Reuben scooted forward and interjected. "We both admire how you're raising your girls. We can't think of anyone else we

trust as much as we trust the two of you. So we'd like to … well
…." He put his hand on Rebecca's knee. "We'd like to draw up
something legal."

"You know," Rebecca waved her hand dismissively in
an attempt to downplay their request, "for any worst-case
scenarios."

Mike nodded. "I understand. We've made the same
arrangements with my brother and his wife. It's a smart thing
to do."

*   *   *

While Mike kept talking with Rebecca and Reuben, Kate
focused on the mug of tea cradled in her hands. She watched
the warm liquid move as she tilted it one way, then another.
She needed a moment to sort her scrambled feelings before
she could respond to their request. For the past few months,
she had felt increasingly aggravated about being caught in the
middle. Between her mom and dad, and between her mom
and Rebecca. She found herself constantly on guard during her
individual conversations with each of them so that she could
quickly circumvent any potential mention of the other. She was
tired of this.

Forget all of the legal issues. She couldn't even go there.
What about the day-to-day events? She could already feel the
tension in her stomach just picturing her mom happily walking
in here, ready to visit the girls, only to encounter Rebecca and

her baby cozied-up on Kate's couch. She tried to imagine her mother's reaction if Naomi and Fiona spent the day at Rebecca's house. Why couldn't they just figure out how to get along? Why was this always on her?

But she couldn't say no. Rebecca meant everything to her. In many ways, she felt closer to her than to her mom. She could never explain it, even to herself. From as far back as she could remember, she and Rebecca just lit up when they saw each other. It wasn't very often when she was little, of course, since Martha avoided Rebecca most of the time. But Kate recalled a number of holiday gatherings when her grandparents were still alive. Rebecca came to those. And what fun the two of them had then, playing simple games before dinner, and Rebecca reading to her. When Rebecca moved to northern California, Kate had felt devastated. But they wrote letters, Kate often included some artwork, and her dad helped her mail them.

When she was in middle school, her grandparents died about two years apart, and Rebecca came for the funerals. They had a little bit of time to visit then. Kate poured out her teen angst to Rebecca and found her to be a loving, listening ear. Sure, her parents were loving to her, too. But sometimes you need a non-parent to help you sort things out.

Why couldn't those two figure out how to get along?

Rebecca broke into her thoughts. "Katie, I know this really puts you in a spot with your mom."

Kate looked up and smiled at her aunt. "It's all right, Becca," she said. "I think it's a great plan."

*   *   *

Martha hit the Off button of her phone as hard as her thumb could jab. At times like this, she wished that she had an old-fashioned phone with a receiver that she could slam down. That was always so much more satisfying when she was angry. A rush of energy buzzed in Martha's head, making loops that seemed to vibrate around her brain. It was bad enough to hear this at all, but to find out from Naomi, a four-year-old who happened to let it slip! And only because she had called, and Naomi answered. "Guess what, Grammy?" Naomi had said. "Auntie Rebecca and Uncle Reuben are having a baby!" How long would Kate have waited to tell her? She sure didn't give Martha any good answers when she got on the line. *Why does Kate let herself get hooked into Rebecca's life? How can she do this to me?*

Still glaring at the exasperatingly modern phone in her other hand, a knock on the back door startled her. She strode to the door and whipped it open to find her new neighbor, Isabelle, hugging a stack of books. Isabelle's black curly hair framed her face in wild wisps.

"Hi, Martha, thanks so much for these. They were a big help."

Martha stared at her, trying to change gears and finding it difficult. Her brows knitted together in a deep V.

"Are you okay?" Isabelle asked warily.

"Hi, Isabelle. Sorry. Come on in."

Isabelle entered and put the books on the kitchen table. She had bought the house next door a few months earlier, after the death of old Jewell Peabody. Jewell had had no relatives and had been sick for many years, leaving the paint to peel, vines to overgrow the house, and the grass to dry out in stickery tufts, making the whole block—in Martha's opinion—look ratty. So Martha was thrilled that Isabelle wanted to fix it up, and happily lent her several landscaping and decorating books. She helped Isabelle paint her living room (Creamy Mushroom) two weeks ago. They enjoyed their time, working, talking, and sharing lunch.

Martha still gripped the phone, scowling at it. Isabelle watched her for a moment and then scanned the kitchen while she waited. Stark white walls contrasted with black granite countertops. Black-and-white checkered linoleum and stainless steel appliances tied it all together. The white-framed glass cupboard doors showed every dish and glass neatly arranged. Bright red towels, oven mitts, and canisters accented the room. "I've probably said this before," Isabelle said, "but I sure admire your bold decor."

Martha shook her head as if awakening. "What?"

"Are you okay?" Isabelle asked again.

Martha huffed loudly. "Augh! I'm sorry. No, I guess I'm really not. I just got off the phone with my daughter, Kate. My sister, Rebecca, is pregnant! Augh!" she growled again. She pointedly banged the phone onto the counter as firmly as she dared; these stupid things could crack.

"Um … is that bad?"

"Oh! It's unbelievable! What was she thinking? What is she going to do? I can't believe she's doing this! And with *him*! How can she be so insane?"

"Um, I don't understand."

Martha sighed deeply, then suddenly focused more directly on Isabelle. "You want some coffee?"

"Sure."

Martha filled a clear glass kettle with filtered water, turned on the burner, then dug into a cupboard under the counter and pulled out a black ceramic canister. She scooped out dark beans and poured them into a little grinder, hitting Pulse over and over, her lips pursed. She pulled off the lid, inspected the grounds. "Damn! Too fine!" she cursed. She dumped the grounds into the trash and scooped again. *Pulse, pulse, pulse.* She inspected it again with a suspicious squint. Isabelle watched her, but kept quiet. Martha poured the perfect coarse grounds into a crystal-clear French press.

"My sister has always been contrary," she railed at the teakettle as it worked its way to a boil. "She has to fly in the face of the rest of us. Where does she get off?" She turned around and leaned against the counter next to the stove. "Sorry, Isabelle. I don't mean to be so crabby. I'm glad you came over."

Isabelle leaned against the opposite counter. "Actually, I didn't realize you had a sister," she ventured.

"Well, she's younger than me. She was the baby, so everyone spoiled her. I think that's what went wrong. No one held her accountable. I'm two years older than her. We have a brother, too, who is three years older than me. He lives in Vermont. We're not in touch all that often. But Rebecca lives in Berkeley again, after being gone for many years."

Martha watched the kettle, pulling it off the heat when the tiniest bubbles started to form. She poured the water into the French press. "You have to catch the water just before it boils, or you'll scorch the flavor," she instructed Isabelle.

"Wow. How did you become such an expert at this?"

"Oh, there's a book for everything."

"So tell me about Rebecca. What happened?"

"First of all, she divorced the nicest man in the world for no reason!" Martha's eyes flickered all around the room. She blew out a breath and declared, "I have to clean the bathroom. But I could use the company. You want to come and talk to me?"

"Sure. Can I help?"

"No, just talk to me."

Martha threw an apron over her slim designer jeans and T-shirt, dug under her sink for the bucket of supplies, and strode into the hallway. Isabelle followed, with a backward glance at the abandoned French press.

"Okay, it's sort of complicated." Martha snapped on her rubber gloves, then stood over the bathtub and sprinkled cleanser into it. She added a bit of water, grabbed a rag, and started to spread the gritty lather around. "Rebecca was married to Ted—he really *was* the nicest man in the world, and a stable accountant. Greg and I both liked him. She was lucky to get him."

Isabelle put the toilet lid down and sat. Even there, she had to lean away from the flying cleanser as Martha continued.

"At first, everything was great. Then all of a sudden, Rebecca ups and divorces Ted. Says she wasn't happy, though for the life of me I couldn't imagine why. Ted was heartbroken. Greg and I had him over for dinner a lot to console him, but we had nothing to say to her. Anyway, after a few years, she moved up north to Yonah River and you know what they're like up there."

"Um, no, actually I don't," Isabelle replied apologetically.

"Oh, right; you're new to California. Well, Yonah River is like the hippie capital of the world now. If you want to know what happened to all those aging hippies from the sixties, that's where they are, in the middle of the redwood forest. She's a biology teacher, and she got a job at a high school up there." Martha began wiping the tile shower walls, then stopped to inspect her work. She tossed the rag on the tub floor, grabbed a stiff brush, made a cleanser paste, and started in on the grout around each tile. She stepped up on the edge of the tub to reach the high corners and work her way down.

"Meanwhile, my friend Cathy, who I knew from our community soccer team, had two boys about the same age as Kate, so our kids had a lot of playdates together. Then one day, Cathy's husband, Reuben, suddenly moved out, and the next thing you know he's got a girlfriend—an artist from New York. The sleazeball. Cathy was heartbroken. So she hung out over here a lot with me on our days off, and the kids—my daughter, Kate, and her boys, Jeffrey and Ben—played together more often than ever. Of course, Ted was around here a lot, so I guess it's no surprise that not much time passed before Cathy and Ted started dating, and eventually got married."

"Wow! That's wild!"

"I know, isn't it? And it speaks well of them that they made something good out of a disaster. They're both such good, stable people. I'm so glad they found someone they can rely on. They deserve to be happy."

"So, Rebecca is in Berkeley now, not Yonah River?"

"Correct. She moved back here a few years ago when she got a job with some weird alternative high school. I thought I wouldn't need to see her anymore after our parents died, but she's weaseled her way into Kate's life. So now if I want to see my own daughter and granddaughters, I have to run into Rebecca now, too, or else work around her schedule."

Martha make a kind of spitting noise, then continued.

"Then! This is unbelievable. Then! No one had the decency to tell me this until Rebecca had been back in town for almost a year, but Reuben and Rebecca have been seeing each other for the last three years! And now she's pregnant! Two of the most irresponsible people on the planet, and now they're going to have a baby! This is just one more of her antics that I have to deal with!" Martha got down on her knees on the bath rug and took the brush to the bottom of the tub. Her earrings jostled with her scrubbing.

Isabelle crossed her legs, then uncrossed them. She rested her chin in her hand. "So how old are they?"

"Ugh!" Martha threw the brush down. "That's just it! Rebecca is forty-nine years old! What kind of age is that to start having babies? And Reuben is fifty-two, going on *thirteen*."

She picked up the brush again and went at the sides of the tub.

"Wow. That's got to be scary, starting a family at that age."

Martha stopped cleaning and looked at her.

"I mean," Isabelle speculated, "if I were her, I'd be really scared. Wouldn't you?"

Martha stayed quiet a moment. "I wouldn't get myself into that situation."

"Right. But, well, I wonder. I mean, if it were *me*. Well, I'd probably need some moral support. Do you think maybe Rebecca is hoping for that?"

Martha turned back to her scrubbing.

*   *   *

June

Now that she was into her fourth month, the morning sickness had retreated, and Rebecca felt a new energy and sense of well-being. She enjoyed hikes in Tilden Park with Reuben and walks at the dog park with Ellen and Brutus. She felt well enough to teach half-day summer school and had her afternoons free to rest and commune with her garden. At times, she paused in surprise at how she had changed from having no interest in being domestic, to this state of contentment.

Friends began to comment that she "glowed." This and the fact that she had made it past twelve weeks encouraged her to tell them that she was, indeed, pregnant—news that stunned them at first. Fortunately, she found that she had no interest in their reaction or advice. Instead, a new feeling of wonderment took over as she became more aware that a life was growing inside her. She had never dreamed it possible to feel this kind of joy.

Her baby bump became round and firm, while her breasts grew heavy and tender. She could feel the baby's movements across her uterine wall. Reuben diligently monitored the stages of pregnancy—in Ann's approved book, not online. Now that the baby's hearing was already well developed, he talked to the baby every evening, with his hand on Rebecca's belly. Sometimes he said silly things, but usually he spoke in soft, confidential tones while Rebecca watched. Sometimes he made Rebecca laugh; always she felt waves of gratitude for him. With the morning sickness gone, her sex drive had returned. She felt grateful that her anxiety had mostly faded into the background, and this was a wonderful time for them both.

Rebecca finished sweeping out the studio in her basement. Her renter had just moved out after graduating from the university, leaving a good space for Reuben's office furniture. Now that Reuben's boys were on their own—Jeffrey in San Jose and Ben in Santa Cruz—he had told her he didn't feel unduly attached to his house. In spite of his casual stance, she knew how much work he had put into his house and landscaping, and she hoped he wouldn't miss it too much.

She went out to the front yard to sweep the walk. Jeffrey and Ben pulled up in the U-Haul behind their dad's car and hopped out. Jeffrey wore jeans and a brown T-shirt that said "National Sarcasm Society: Like we need your support." He wore heavy black-rimmed glasses, and his dark brown buzz cut only allowed a hint of his naturally wavy hair. Reuben got out of his car and went straight the U-Haul to start unpacking.

"Becca," Jeffrey gave her a hug.

"Hey," she hugged him back. "Thanks for helping out today, guys."

"No problem," said Ben, coming over to hug her. His straight, dark blonde hair covered his forehead at a diagonal. His purple T-shirt over khaki cargo pants had the *Om* sign in dark green followed by a capital *G*. "You got anything to eat?" he asked her.

Reuben looked up from working the truck latch. "What? You just got here!"

Rebecca smiled. "We'll be right back!" she called over her shoulder, as she took Ben's elbow conspiratorially and headed for the house. Jeffrey followed, grinning back at Reuben.

"At least carry something in! Don't waste a trip!" Reuben shouted futilely, and shook his head. "I swear." He swung open the back doors of the truck and started unloading boxes himself.

Mark parked his car and came over to help. "You still need a renter for your house?"

"Yeah." Reuben handed him a box.

"I think I've got a lead for you."

The sun shone its last rays across the sky as Rebecca stepped into the backyard. The moving completed for the day, Reuben had set up his large mesh hammock on the small patio next to the house, the only area he could find that wouldn't interfere with Rebecca's plants. Rebecca found him there, stretched out with his eyes closed.

"Hey," she grinned at him.

"Hey!" He scooted over. "Come on in." He lifted his arm to make a space for her.

Rebecca wobbled the hammock as she sat, swung her legs around, and snuggled next to him, head on his shoulder.

"So," he said. "Just another week or so for the ultrasound?"

"Yep."

"Have you thought about names, or do you want to wait until we know the gender?" he asked.

Rebecca lifted her head and chuckled at him. "Ah, your mind has been busy."

He gave her a sheepish smile.

"Well," Rebecca shifted in the hammock, lifting her long braid out of the way. "It's probably a good idea to toss around some names now, just to get warmed up. Do you have any you like?"

"I want it to be something different enough that it's not duplicated with other kids in school," Reuben said. "That's a pain. But I don't want it to be so unusual that people struggle with pronouncing it or spelling it all the time."

"So, what's different, but pronounceable?" Rebecca scanned her mind for characters in books, movies, and TV shows.

"Nobody famous," she said. "Or goofy." Then she smiled. "For instance, you can't name a girl Endora, for heaven's sake."

Reuben suddenly laughed, coughing with surprise.

"Or if it's a boy," she continued, "It can't be Gilligan. I'm putting my foot down about that."

Reuben guffawed now and leaned away from Rebecca to cough, then back to hug her. The hammock lurched wildly. They both grabbed the edges to steady it as it rocked and dipped.

*   *   *

Martha paced her kitchen, watching the clock. She wore high heels, a kelly green skirt with a yellow blouse, green necklace, and bracelet. Matching earrings dangled below her highlighted pixie cut. "Where is he?" she said through gritted teeth, not for the first time.

Kate, also dressed for the reception, sat at the kitchen table in a blue floral skirt and pullover sweater. "Mom, he'll be here. He promised. There was probably a long line at the hardware store."

"Why does he have to wait 'til the last minute? He knows this is library expansion is important to me! Why can't he—"

The door opened and Greg came in. Dropping bags on the table, he walked over to the kitchen sink, rolled up the sleeves of his work shirt, and started to wash his hands.

Martha assessed him from head to toe. "We don't have a lot of time. We're supposed to be there in half an hour."

"I'll be ready."

"Why don't you just wash your hands while you take a shower?"

"I need to eat something first."

"They're serving appetizers!"

"I need real food."

Kate bent down, pretending to search for something in her purse. She hated listening to them argue. She wanted to leave, but didn't want to add to the scene. *Shit. Here we go again.* She pulled out an emery board and concentrated on filing her nails.

Martha huffed at Greg. "This means a lot to me. I've worked hard on this project, and I want you to meet the people I've sweated with—over the bureaucracies, the creative ideas, *everything.* I want to share this with you, and you act like you don't even want to be there. How do you think that makes me feel?"

"I'll be ready on time. Just relax."

"Don't tell me to relax!" Pink blotches spread up her neck to her cheeks. "Why can't you just *care*, even *one time*, about what I do? I go to all of *your* events, and all you do is flirt with other women, leaving me to entertain myself." She halted for a moment, seeming to consider this. Greg said nothing.

Kate slung her purse over her shoulder and stood. "You know, I think I'll just meet you guys there."

"Kate! No, honey," Martha's voice wobbled. "Don't go."

"Mom," Kate paused. *What in the world could she say?* "Mom," she faced Martha squarely and tried to keep her voice steady. "I can't be here for such a personal discussion. I'm *going* to meet you at the reception."

Martha glared at Greg, who, oblivious, rummaged in the refrigerator.

Kate turned and slipped out the door.

*   *   *

July

Reuben clicked off the TV. His head resting on the back of the couch, he glanced at Rebecca. "You ready for tomorrow?"

"I'm excited to find out if it's a boy or a girl." She paused. "And anything else we can learn." She fell silent.

He turned toward her and touched her arm. "How are you doing?"

She studied her palms before turning to Reuben. "I'm scared." Saying this aloud caused a few tears to appear. For most of her life, she had hardly ever cried. Now, these days, she couldn't believe how often it happened. She shook her head for a moment with this fleeting observation but continued her train of thought with Reuben. "I've mostly been doing well lately, but I have this unsteady feeling going on under the surface—this fear—that's there all the time. I don't know what we're going to find out tomorrow. I don't know how the baby is going to be." She sniffed, and her words tumbled out more quickly now. "I don't know if I have the stamina to give birth, or recover from it! I don't know if I can be a good mom. I look at families I've known, personally or through school, and I see over and over again how people just repeat the patterns of their parents, even if they don't mean to. I'm afraid of getting too tired and slipping into impatience or even anger, like my dad used to. And my mom was so detached. I never had a good role model. I don't know how to act. I don't want to screw up this kid. Growing up, I was so lonesome and scared. I don't want to do that to my baby. But most of all, I don't know if the baby will even be born healthy." She took a shaky breath. "I don't know if my baby will be okay." The tears fell now, much harder than Rebecca had expected. Reuben's arms wrapped around her, and she leaned into him. Her nose smushed against his chest and she didn't care. She grabbed his flannel shirt with both hands and hung on. Reuben held onto her and pivoted them both around so they could lie on the couch.

"It'll be okay," he said, stroking her face. "You're strong. You're amazing. Even though I know this, I never stop being impressed with your stamina on hikes, and you know how much I admire how great you are with your students. I mean, you are *terrific* with them. I can't imagine you not being at least as nurturing with your own kid. You've obviously thought a lot over the years about healthy behavior. When people make a conscious choice, they don't have to repeat history. I know I made plenty of mistakes with my boys, but we've gotten through it and we're good. And in my teaching, hell, I know that sometimes I've been less than tactful with my students. But I'm not going to cash it in and go flip burgers just because I failed to be Gandhi. I mean, *overall,* I think I've done okay by them. You can't expect yourself to be perfect. No one can do that." She kept frowning. "And Becca," now Reuben made a point of looking directly into her eyes. "You know I'm here. I'm *here*. You won't be doing this alone."

Rebecca answered by holding him closer. They lay in silence for a while, and she felt her breathing slow and deepen. The panic passed, though that now-familiar anxiety remained a steady undercurrent. Even so, this was better than she had felt all week. Just feeling calmer for the moment made her want to stay right there in that position forever; maybe it would keep the panic away indefinitely. But after a while, the narrowness of the couch couldn't be ignored, and Reuben's arm was asleep. They groggily clambered up and, hanging on to each other, staggered down the hall and fell into bed. And though they tried not to disturb each other, neither slept well.

Rebecca and Reuben held hands and watched the monitor in wonder as Shankar, the sonographer, passed the transducer over Rebecca's gel-covered belly. "Okay, so far your baby likes to have its picture taken," he said. "This is nice and clear. You want to know the gender?"

"Yes," Rebecca said. Her voice was quieter than she meant it to be. Shankar glanced at Reuben, who nodded.

Shankar slid the transducer one way, then the other. He pressed it firmly at the sides of Rebecca's lower belly, held it for a moment, then slid it a bit farther. "I'm trying to find just the right angle," he explained. Finally, he held one position, pointed to the monitor that showed what looked at first like a grey blurry mass. "Congratulations," he smiled. "It's a girl."

Tears sprang from Rebecca's eyes (*there go those tears again; oh, well*), surprising her with joy and relief. She felt Reuben's beard press on her cheek as he hugged her, then kissed her head. They watched their baby wiggle from side to side as Shankar moved the instrument again. He freeze-framed various angles, showing the size of the baby, major organs, the condition of the placenta, and Rebecca's cervix. Then he set the handset down and swabbed the gel from Rebecca's belly.

"Okay, you're done," he said. "You can get dressed. You can see Alayna up front. She'll give you the pictures to take with you."

"Thank you so much." Reuben shook his hand.

"You're very welcome," Shankar smiled. "Congratulations, again," he said, and he left.

"I'll get the pictures and see you out there," Reuben said to Rebecca.

"Okay," she said as he shut the door. She was preoccupied with finding some tissues to wipe off the gooey gel that remained on her belly. Still sticky. She grabbed some paper towels, which she ran under the faucet, and cleaned up a bit more. *It's a girl!* She smiled a big smile to herself. She would have been happy with either gender, but she found herself giddy at the thought of cuddling a little girl.

But with a sudden shift, she felt a little dizzy. *There really is a baby on the way.* She felt like she was entering an alternate universe. She sat down on a plastic chair and waited, as if this quiet room that had just miraculously revealed the gender of her baby could also endow her with some navigational chart she could depend on.

*　　　　*　　　　*

The receptionist handed Reuben a stack of pictures. "These are your copies, and we'll send another set to your doctor."

Reuben thanked her and walked toward a chair while paging through the pictures. *A girl!* He sat and pored over the images from various angles, trying to make out what the main focus might be. It wasn't easy to see much, but these things were clearer than when the boys were on their way. *Now I'm doing it again. Holy crap. This is real!*

*　　　　*　　　　*

August

Reuben circled the block again, searching for a parking place for their first childbirth class. Rebecca had been quiet, unable to get comfortable all the way there. If it's this bad now, after only six months, what's it going to be like in November? she wondered, shifting her weight once again. "Just pace yourself," Ann had said the other day as she checked Rebecca's blood pressure yet again. "Eat small amounts, but eat often, and drink lots of water. You're doing fine. Just pace yourself. Stretch. Breathe."

Stretch? Already she felt like a whale, struggling to walk on land, bumping into furniture and doorjambs, as her bruises proved. She had swollen ankles, backaches, leg cramps, headaches, and felt too hot all the time.

"It's a miracle any woman does this more than once," she said to Reuben, as he finished parking the car and set the brake.

He took her hand and kissed it. A month ago, she would have loved this. But now she couldn't wait for him to take his lips off her. When he leaned over to kiss her on the mouth, she pulled back. She had always loved getting close to the soft spice scent that his soap left on his skin, but now it made her stomach reel. He stopped and sighed, resting against the seatback. "Okay, you ready?" he asked.

"I guess."

They walked into the clinic's classroom. Five couples were already there, getting settled among the many large pillows scattered over the wall-to-wall carpeting. Rebecca hesitated at the door and scanned the room. She was old enough to be the mother of every person there, maybe including the teacher, too. What was she doing here?

And how was she going to get back up off the floor, once she got down there?

September

Rebecca lay awake again, listening to Reuben's soft snore. Since school started last week, she'd been tired from trying to keep up with her usual intense focus and pace in the classroom. Ann had expressed concern about the recent rise in Rebecca's blood pressure. She really needed a good night's sleep, but no matter what position she heaved herself into next, it wouldn't help. Her back ached, and for some reason she had carpal tunnel syndrome in both wrists, which made no sense to her. She felt agitated, remembering the unwelcome encounter when she took a walk around her block that afternoon. Lost in thought as she walked, she hadn't seen Della, the neighborhood drama queen, talking with another woman directly in Rebecca's path until it was too late to avoid her. Della had asked how she was feeling. Rebecca knew better than to say anything beyond "great!" but without provocation, Della and her friend launched into stories about bizarre, disastrous things that had happened during other women's pregnancies. Rebecca hastily told them she had to go and walked on as quickly as she could, to their surprised silence, though she could hear that they picked up again on the same thread only a moment later. *What in the hell possesses people to tell horror stories like that?* Rebecca fumed now in bed. *How could that be remotely helpful to anyone?* She blew out an exasperated blast of air. "People suck!" she growled into the darkness, louder than she meant to.

Reuben jolted awake, disoriented.

October

All of Rebecca's students were gone for the day except for Gina, who sat at a table making up the test that she had missed. The chartreuse streaks in her jet-black hair hung over her face as she worked. She sat back and surveyed her diagrams, fingering the multiple piercings in her ears. Bent forward again, she finished her labeling (*cell membrane, chloroplasts, endoplasmic reticulum, golgi bodies, mitochondria, nucleolus, ribosomes, vacuole*) and drew in the finishing touches on her illustrations. Gina, an artist at heart, Rebecca thought, clearly enjoyed adding as many details as she could to the diagrams—her favorite part of the test. She sharpened the pencil with her hand-held sharpener many times before she was done, brushing the fine shavings off her black knit sleeve that had a thumbhole cut out so that the sleeve covered half of her hand. Usually she wore black pants and shoes, too, but today, hiking boots peeked out from under her long A-line denim skirt covered with bleach-applied stars. Rebecca was glad that Gina had become more comfortable expressing herself. She'd known her for two years now. This was what she loved about an alternative high school that had only forty students and five teachers: so much more opportunity to get to know each other, more chances to follow through and find out how things turned out for each kid.

She thought about the baby growing inside her. What was her daughter going to be like? Would she fit in at a regular high school, or would she feel rejected by the mainstream like Gina did? Rebecca's heart ached for children who had to contend with social challenges at school. And would her baby have any learning disabilities? Would she find it hard to stay focused? Would she be the least bit interested in school? Would she even be speaking to Rebecca by the time she was in high school? Could Rebecca avoid her own parents' pitfalls?

"I think that's it, Ms. T.," Gina said, getting up to hand the paper to Rebecca.

Rebecca took the paper. "Great. How do you feel about how you did?"

"I'm good with it," Gina nodded. "I love this stuff, so I think I remembered everything."

"Excellent. I'm glad you're feeling better. Nice to have you back."

Gina picked up her satchel. "Thanks. See you tomorrow." She hesitated, then set her satchel on the table. "So, Ms. T., have you decided yet when your last day will be?"

"I'm getting closer to deciding, Gina. I'm not due 'til early November, but I want to find a good time for the sub to start with you guys; that will make the shift easier for everyone. I'm thinking maybe at the end of the quarter, which is just around the corner."

Gina dropped her eyes. "Do you know yet who the sub will be?"

"Not yet, but I'm working on getting someone good who can appreciate what brilliant students I have." Gina looked up, and Rebecca smiled at her. "I'll let you know as soon as I find out."

"So, are you feeling okay?"

"Yes. I'm tired, and I feel way too huge and clumsy, but I'm okay. I'll bet it's odd for you all to see an old teacher pregnant."

"It did kind of surprise us the first day of school, but, well, you know, you're in the right place. I mean, if this were a regular high school, it would be all effed-up social rejection, but here, um … no offense, Ms. T., but you already know … this is the haven for misfits." Gina squinted at Rebecca, smiling tentatively. When Rebecca laughed, she laughed too.

"Gina, you just made my day. I mean it." Rebecca, still laughing, struggled out of her chair and gave Gina a hug.

November

Rebecca folded and refolded the little flannel sheets, rearranged tiny baby outfits in the dresser drawers, and gently tapped the smiling faces on the mobile above the changing table, making them bob up and down. Now that she was off work, her days felt lonely with everyone else she knew at their own jobs. She tried reading, but she found it hard to concentrate, and besides, she could never get comfortable. This morning she had walked around the block, hoping that this would loosen up her discomfort. By now she was used to the ligaments in her hip area hurting when she walked too far or too fast, but the dull aching squeezes she'd experienced before had never been quite as low in her abdomen as this. It was a beautiful day, with a clear blue sky and crisp air, but she couldn't enjoy it as much as she had hoped.

This week, she had felt increasingly frustrated about her

discomfort. Fortunately, today Kate, Naomi, and Fiona had come over for lunch, which had been a welcome distraction. The highlight of the visit occurred when the baby had an especially wild kicking session. Naomi and Fiona were able to feel it as they gently held their little hands on her belly, wide-eyed. She took a nap afterward (Ann had encouraged her to store up as much energy as she could between now and the birth), but now things were too quiet again.

She scanned the baby's room, as if anything could have eluded her notice during previous inspections. She stopped at the photo of herself and Reuben on the dresser. She thought of her parents. Did they stand in her room before she was born, wondering who their new baby might be? Or were they already too occupied with her brother and sister to be able to think about her? Did they want her, or was she a surprise? What was it like for them to have her arrive? Was her father already the angry sullen person she experienced, or did that happen after she was born? Had her mother always been distant? What would motherhood do to Rebecca?

What about Reuben's parents? she wondered. What had it been like for them to anticipate his birth? Did they stand in his room and speculate the way she and Reuben did in here some evenings? Reuben said they had always been supportive of him and his brother and sister. Now she wished she'd had a chance to get to know his mom before she died. At least his dad would be around to hold the baby and play with her. She felt grateful that her baby would have at least one grandparent, and a supportive one at that.

Then she remembered that when she was little, Lydia, the

elderly woman next door, had been a kind of a grandmother to her. Maybe someone like that would come into her baby's life.

She practiced her relaxation exercises for a few minutes. Even those didn't relieve the achiness that came and went. She needed some distraction. She grabbed her purse and headed for the door. Today was the farmer's market on Rose Street— the perfect place to stroll and sample goodies. It was only four-thirty, plenty of time to get there and enjoy all the colors and flavors before they closed.

The beet greens looked especially appealing today with their dark green, red-veined leaves—not ragged, as they often were. She chose a large bunch, chatted with the woman in the booth for a minute, and selected some nice zucchini before continuing on. Ah, here was that friendly Israeli man who loved to give out samples of his hummus on pita. She could use a snack.

"Ms. T!" called a voice behind her.

Rebecca turned around. "Carlos!" she greeted her student.

Carlos, a senior at Rebecca's school, walked over with two other boys who appeared to be a few years younger than him. They had the same broad smile that Carlos did.

"Hey, Ms. T! How's it going?"

"I'm doing fine, Carlos; how about you?"

"Good. We're getting veggies for our mom." He held up full bags. "Ms. T., these are my brothers, Francisco and Hector."

The boys nodded, and each reached out a hand. Carlos and Hector wore jeans and T-shirts, and their hair was tousled, but Francisco (probably about fifteen, Rebecca guessed) had on black chinos, a snug red T-shirt, and his hair was slicked back.

Rebecca shook their hands. "Nice to meet you both."

"Our mom usually gets the veggies," Hector said. "But Francisco here is in love with the girl at the flower stall, so he volunteered."

Francisco smacked his younger brother on the shoulder. "Go take a walk; go do something somewhere," he scolded, his face flushing.

"Okay, okay." Carlos put his hand on Francisco's shoulder, then turned to Rebecca. "So, the sub is okay, but it's kind of boring without you there, Ms. T."

"Are you working hard for him?"

"Of course!" He smiled his most charming smile at her. Then he became more serious. "I sent in the scholarship applications, like you told me."

"Oh, I'm glad, Carlos. I look forward to hearing who responds first." She paused, feeling another ache grow larger within. *It's nothing*, she thought to herself. But the ache gripped Rebecca—hard. Her face flinched as she grabbed her belly.

Concern flashed across Carlos's face. "You okay?"

Rebecca let out a long breath. "I'm fine. It's just, you know, a pregnancy thing. I'd better get on home. It's been a full day. Keep working hard," she half-groaned before turning to leave.

"I will. Bye, Ms. T.," Carlos waved and moved away hesitantly. His brothers waved at her too, and moved on more quickly than their older brother to the next booth. Francisco smacked Hector's shoulder one more time, only to be answered with Hector's mocking laughter.

Rebecca held her lower back with one hand and waddled toward her car. Suddenly, a larger pain gripped her belly, this time pressing sharply into her tailbone. "Oh!" She dropped her bags and buckled forward, clutching her belly. A man and a woman ran to her side, followed seconds later by Carlos and his brothers.

As she caught her breath and righted herself, she attempted to smile at Carlos, because the worry on his face looked like it could turn to horror. She tried to say something reassuring but found no words would come. She leaned on the nearest booth and tried to think, but couldn't shake a feeling of dread.

Already she felt another squeeze creeping up on her. It reminded her of the menstrual cramps she used to have. But now, as the pain gripped her belly tighter and tighter, it was as if nine months of missing cramps had banded together and decided to attack at once. When she thought it couldn't get worse, the vice tightened further and Rebecca dropped to her knees.

Now she was surrounded by a flurry of concerned voices and a barrage of questions, kind hands gentle on her back. It sounded like a lot of people, but all Rebecca could see were her own hands, flat against the asphalt. At this point, she didn't care what she looked like; she stayed on her hands and knees and focused on her hands, there: there on the ground. The nauseating ache in her stomach suddenly gripped her lower back, too, and she heard herself emit something between a whimper and a moan.

In the height of such internal intensity, she felt her body contract as if it wasn't under her control. Something pushed hard against the floor of her pelvis.

Then slowly, blessedly, the pain began to subside. Rebecca could breathe again; the blur of sound and movement around her came back into sharper focus. The pain receded more, and Rebecca thought she might cry with relief. All she could think was that she didn't want that feeling to come back.

She began to feel like herself again, but as she did, the noise of the market sounded suddenly deafening, and the smell from the pretzel booth nauseated her.

"I've got to get out of here," she heard herself say aloud from deep inside some kind of echoing tunnel. Other voices said something, and she responded with something else, but it all sounded blurry to her.

Arms reached, helped her up; a woman locked Rebecca's bags of vegetables in Rebecca's car. More questions. "No, no, it's fine, I know him; Carlos can do it," she heard herself say. The woman helped her into Carlos's car, somehow managed to get a seatbelt around her. Strangers receded; the engine roared. She concentrated on breathing, fumbled for her phone. *Call Reuben, call Ann, call Ellen, inhale, exhale, think of a peaceful beach, Reuben, Reuben, I'm on my way, keep calling Ann, inhale. Beach. Soft breeze. Exhale.*

She couldn't turn her body to check; she assumed that Carlos's brothers were in the back seat, though it was completely silent back there.

"Hang in there, Ms. T.; we've got you covered," Carlos offered.

Oh, great. Just think of what the kids are going to be talking about in school tomorrow.

Exhaustion permeated Rebecca's body. Her face hot and sweaty, she felt the latest violent contraction subside, knowing the relief was only temporary. Ann checked her blood pressure again, looking more businesslike than Rebecca had ever seen her. Something was wrong; Rebecca just knew it. Of course. Why wouldn't there be? Ann had tried to prepare her for the possibility that she would want to speed the labor along if she became too exhausted. Specialists whose titles Rebecca couldn't remember had already come in to meet her and ask her questions, to prepare in case they were suddenly needed. She couldn't explain it, but she found this more frightening than if no help were available.

With the next contraction, she grabbed onto Reuben's arm. He put his hand on hers. "You're doing okay; you're doing great, Becca."

Her hospital gown was soaked now. She felt like she'd been doing this for days, though this couldn't be true. *Could it?* She felt lost in timelessness. "I can't do this anymore," she surrendered in a hoarse voice.

Ann, seated at the foot of the delivery bed, took only a moment to analyze Rebecca's face. "Okay," she said. She pressed a button on the wall and continued to watch Rebecca and the monitors.

Orchid, the nurse, stepped closer to comfort her. Orchid was from Jamaica. Rebecca had found the cadence of her soft, low voice especially soothing earlier, as Orchid told her stories about her own children and grandchildren. When she learned about Rebecca's garden, she described flowers that she had grown up with in Jamaica. Ginger lily, kiss me over the garden gate, sandalwood bramble, and—her personal favorite—Moses in a basket: soft reddish-purple pods, with tiny cream-colored flowers peeking out. In this way, Orchid managed to distract Rebecca from her discouragement. Rebecca had listened hungrily, savoring the calming effect this had on her. But now nothing helped. Rebecca felt herself whimper.

Orchid put her soft strong hands on Reuben's shoulders, and sat him down in the chair next to the bed. She gave him a maternal pat on the cheek before turning her back on him and taking Rebecca's hand and massaging it. "Make those sounds low and open from your belly, darling," she directed Rebecca, stroking her forehead.

Rebecca groaned loudly as another contraction rolled in. As it climaxed, she felt something change within her. Instead of dread, she felt determination. As the familiar urge to push bore down on her, she knew. She had to push this baby out, no matter what happened to her. She had to.

Orchid must have felt the change in Rebecca too. She looked at Ann.

Two men in scrubs entered, one wheeling in a table with some equipment on it that Rebecca didn't recognize.

"No!" she yelled in a booming voice she didn't know she had. "I can do it now!"

With Orchid's help, Rebecca sat up and leaned forward as the next contraction came before the last one had even stopped. She pushed against the pain, channeling it out of her body. She heard Reuben's voice next to her again. "You're doing it, Becca; look how strong you are." He wiped her wet hair from her forehead with a towel.

"Okay, just breathe here, Rebecca. I can see the top of her head, but don't push for a moment," Ann directed. "Just breathe."

"You can do it," Reuben said. "You *are* doing it. It's going great."

"Okay, just a small half-push now." She heard Ann's voice, confident. "Her head's out, Becca! You're doing great; you're doing great … you're almost home. On your next contraction, give us a good push."

Rebecca felt the next contraction overtake her, grabbed the bed rails, and pushed.

"Keep pushing, keep pushing," Ann encouraged with her steady voice. "Almost there, a little more …. Here she is!"

Rebecca shouted out and burst into tears through exhausted laughter as others moved the baby's wet body onto her belly. The baby's cry rose above the adult voices and pierced Rebecca's heart.

Reuben, crying and laughing, kissed Rebecca's face, her head, her hand. He pulled his T-shirt up to wipe his face, and found a towel to wipe hers. Rebecca ignored him and reached down to pull her baby to her chest, feeling the slippery, warm umbilical cord still attached, sliding up from between her legs. She caressed her baby. "Welcome, Hannah," she cried softly, laughing, whispering into her ear. "Welcome, little one. My little one."

With Ann's guidance, Rueben cut the umbilical cord. Then he arranged a soft blanket over the baby, tenting her in with Rebecca's warmth, and scooted a chair as close to the bed as he could. Ann bustled around them, suctioning Hannah's nose and throat and Orchid smiled nostalgically at the new family as she whisked used towels and linens out of the way. None of this had any impact on Rebecca, whose eyes were anchored to her baby's.

This human being had been inside her body. She had known that in her brain all this time, but now it felt almost impossible to fathom. "Oh, just look at her!" Rebecca cried at Reuben, whose face was next to hers. "She has your ears." She touched her finger softly to Hannah's ears, outlining them. "And your wonderful hair." Already, wispy brown ringlets covered Hannah's head, which Orchid now covered with a stretchy cotton hat.

Reuben leaned closer to Rebecca's chest to gaze at his daughter. He ran his fingers over her head and stroked her back through the blanket. It took a minute for him to find his voice. He finally said, "Hi, Hannah; I'm your dad."

Hannah shifted her head and faced him directly, as if she recognized his voice.

"Oh, no!" he laughed. "She has that same intense look in

her eyes that you have!" His voice cracked. "I'm a goner!"

Rebecca laughed. Then, overwhelmed with an irresistible pull, Rebecca moved Hannah to her breast. Hannah immediately clamped on, shocking Rebecca with her strong sucking.

Orchid came over with a fresh flannel blanket, and tucked in mother and baby. "Oh, you are a beautiful one, you are," she said to the baby. "And you know your mommy and daddy already love you so much, they don't know what to do with themselves."

Reuben wiped at his joyful tears and stood to give Orchid a hug. She squeezed him back, gave him a few pats, released him, and continued cleaning up. Reuben hugged Ann, whispering his thanks before he returned to Rebecca.

*   *   *

"More champagne?"

"Oh, yes, Thaddeus, thank you!" Rose held up her glass and smiled at Thaddeus. "She made her entrance like a champ, didn't she?"

"Yes she did," he said. "But it's going to be pretty quiet for *us* now."

"Mmm, indeed," Rose nodded. "But it's impossible to be truly sad, isn't it? I mean, look how happy Reuben and Rebecca are." Rose stood next to the towel hamper and gestured toward the couple. "My boy has chosen a wonderful partner. And now I'm a *grandmother* again!" her eyes shone.

Betty and Mahina crossed the room and joined them, holding out their glasses to Thaddeus, who still held the bottle. He poured for them as the women watched the new family.

"I'll miss her," Betty said wistfully.

"So will I," Mahina put her arm around Betty. "She's a scamp, that one. Never a dull moment with her around. But she was ready. Did you see that eager little face as she took her leap?" Mahina's eyes crinkled as she laughed. They all chuckled as they reflected on the memory of just minutes ago.

"I'm still feeling her good-bye hug," said Betty.

"Me too," said Thaddeus. "It was a hearty squeeze, though I think it was the briefest good-bye I've ever gotten. It's like she couldn't wait one more minute."

"No, she couldn't," Mahina agreed.

"Well?" Rose said as she held up her glass. "Here's to the new family!"

"To their new adventure!" Mahina added.

Four glasses clinked.

A colorful shimmer surrounded the friends and they vanished from the room.

*   *   *

Ann placed both hands on her lower back and arched her spine then let out a long exhale. She opened her mouth as if to speak, but, seeing this new family so immersed in each other, she left the room without interrupting them.

She found Ellen and Kate in the waiting area. Ellen had been in the waiting room all night, curled up on the barely padded, very short couch. Kate had gone home to sleep, and had just returned a short while before.

Ann greeted them with a grin. "It is, indeed, a girl," she declared. "Born 8:08 a.m., November 14. Everybody's fine. Rebecca did great, and the baby is nursing already."

Ellen and Kate hugged each other, laughing with newfound energy.

"They're just cleaning up in there," Ann continued, "so give it a few more minutes before you go in. Don't stay too long, though, because they're all really tired. I'll be back soon." She walked stiffly down the hall, her gait gradually loosening.

Reuben, his hair disheveled, came out a few minutes later to invite them in. His gray sweats and white T-shirt were wrinkled, damp, and splotchy, and he had dark circles under his eyes. The second they saw him, Ellen and Kate burst out laughing. "You look terrible!" they said almost at the same time, and Ellen added, "Who gave birth, you, or Rebecca?"

Reuben gave them an exhausted half-smile, and waved them into the room.

*   *   *

Ann returned and sent Kate and Ellen home. It was time for the official baby exam. With other births, she often waited until the next day, but in this case, she wanted to know right away if there was any problem. Rebecca and Reuben were eager to get all of their questions answered, but releasing Hannah, even to Ann, took all the conscious will they had. Ann smiled at them reassuringly and placed Hannah on a towel right on the bed where they could watch every move she made. She unwrapped the blanket from Hannah and slipped off her knit cap. Rebecca reflexively reached out to help. Ann laughed kindly. "It's okay. I've got her."

Rebecca smiled, only slightly embarrassed. "I know that," she said, and reached for Reuben's hand to keep hers busy.

Ann ran her hand all over Hannah's head. She inspected both ears, ran her fingers over Hannah's collarbones, and, in this way, examined every inch down to her toes, pressing gently around her belly. (Rebecca couldn't help leaning forward at this.) Holding Hannah's ankles and wrists, Ann moved the little arms and legs, examined ten fingers, ten toes. She warmed up her stethoscope and listened to the baby's heart. Hannah squirmed and squawked at this. "I can never get this thing warm enough," Ann apologized to Hannah, who eventually settled down again. Reuben squeezed Rebecca's hand and rubbed her arm. Ann listened to Hannah's lungs and her belly, then gently turned her over to check the other side. She ran her thumb down her back just to one side of the spine, then the other. Hannah curved a little toward whichever side the thumb moved on.

"What does *that* mean?" Rebecca worried.

"It's a healthy newborn reflex," Ann said.

Ann grabbed a new diaper, put it on Hannah, then wrapped her expertly in a blanket with special folds and tucks, making sure the baby was snug and warm again. "This is my famous eggroll wrap," she bragged to Hannah. She pulled Hannah's soft cotton hat back onto her head, then stood next to the bed and held her in one arm. With her other hand, she shined a light in Hannah's eyes. She slid one gloved finger into Hannah's mouth, checking her palate and her sucking reflex. Finally, she turned to Rebecca and Reuben. "She's perfect."

Rebecca searched Ann's face carefully. "She's okay? Are you sure?"

"Yes," Ann assured her. "She's got the right number of parts; all of the reflexes we're looking for. You have a healthy baby." She carefully placed Hannah back into Rebecca's outstretched arms.

Rebecca pulled Hannah close to her as relief filled her body. As exhausted as she felt, she couldn't stop staring in wonder at this new life in her arms.

Jeffrey held Hannah carefully, his arms stiff, as he smiled and commented on her tiny features while Reuben stood by. In contrast, when it was his turn, Ben cuddled Hannah and cooed over her. He showed her his repertoire of smiles and funny faces. "Wow, Dad, she's awesome," he said. Reuben put his arm around Ben and they gazed together at the baby.

When Kate and Mike came in with Naomi and Fiona, Ben gingerly handed Hannah over to Kate, who sat down so that Naomi and Fiona could see her. They softly petted her head, then her arms, and talked to her in little falsetto voices. Rebecca watched contentedly for a minute, but soon exhaustion overcame her and she let her eyes close.

They heard a soft knock on the door, as it opened just a little. Greg peeked his face in. "Kate called to tell us that the baby was born," he said to Rebecca. "I hope it's okay that I stopped by."

"Absolutely, Greg," she said when she had recovered from the surprise. "Come on in."

Reuben went over to greet him.

"Oompa!" Naomi called out happily. She took his hand and dragged him away from Reuben. "Come see Hannah!"

December

Rebecca greeted her big brother at the door with a squeal. "I'm *so* glad to see you!" She hugged him tightly.

Brad's lanky frame hunched down to enfold Rebecca in his arms. "Hey, Scruffy," he said, giving her a good long squeeze before releasing her.

Reuben walked over to him, Hannah in his arms. "Hey, Brad," he said.

Brad leaned in close to Hannah. "Lookey here," he said in a higher-than-normal voice.

Reuben started to ease her into Brad's arms.

"Wait!" Rebecca stopped them. "Sorry, Brad, but you've got

to wash your hands first. You've got airport germs all over you."

Brad raised his eyebrows at Reuben in surprise. "This from my little sister who loves to dig in the dirt? The one who says it's good for the soul to get it under your nails?"

"Oops," Reuben shrugged with a sheepish smile at Brad.

"Sorry, big brother, things change," Rebecca said in a kind but determined voice, and gave him a little push down the hall.

"Wow! Okay," Brad said wonderingly as he disappeared into the bathroom.

When he came out, Rebecca happily ushered him to the couch, where Reuben handed Hannah over to him.

"Beer?" Reuben asked.

"That'd be great, thanks."

Reuben left the room as Brad turned to the baby in his arms. He rested her on his lap facing him, keeping her propped up at a slant with both hands. "Hi, Hannah," he said in a gentle lilt. "I'm Uncle Brad."

Hannah blinked somberly at him. He showed her his wide-open eyes, mouth in a big O, then big smiles. When she alternately raised and lowered her little eyebrows, he did the same.

Rebecca sat on the other side of Brad and watched him with an amused smile. "Your hair's gotten grayer," she said. Brad's hair used to be the same chestnut brown as Rebecca's. Now it was more than half silver.

He gave her a mock sneer. "Thanks for pointing that out." But he smiled at his little sister before returning his attention to Hannah. "She's a cutie," he said. "Looks like you, except for the curls. She doing well?"

"Super healthy," Rebecca said proudly.

"How about you?"

"Well, I'm taking a while to recover. It's been more than a month now, and I don't feel like I have all of my energy back yet. My doctor says that's normal; it'll be a while. I kind of challenged my limits."

Brad looked thoughtfully at Rebecca, and said with affection, "You've always taken the unworn path, haven't you?"

Rebecca smiled slightly and shrugged.

"I'm proud of you, Scruffy," he said. "You did good." He turned Hannah and held her next to his chest, supporting her head in the crook of his arm. He lightly rubbed her head; her short curls flipped around under his fingers. His face became pensive. "She's a lucky little girl to have two parents who love her so much," he said. "She'll have a much better childhood than we had."

Rebecca let out a heavy sigh. "I constantly worry about whether I'll be a good enough parent. I'm so afraid of screwing up. Of repeating history."

Reuben returned with beers for Brad and himself, and settled into a chair across from the couch.

"Thanks," Brad said. He turned back to Rebecca. "We've talked about this. We both know what terrible examples we had. But you are perfectly equipped to blaze your own trail. You'll be fine."

Rebecca remained somber. "I hope so." But after a moment, she brightened again. "I'm glad you came. Even though you can't be here for Christmas, I'm glad you're here now. I'm so happy that you'll be with us on Saturday."

"Wouldn't miss it." Brad lifted his beer bottle to both of them and took another sip. "I've been wondering when you guys would do this." He turned back to Hannah and cooed at her. "Isn't it about time?" he asked his brand-new niece in all sincerity.

* * *

Saturday afternoon

The small group broke into applause as Susan, the minister, made the pronouncement and Rebecca and Reuben kissed. Rebecca wore a thin wreath of flowers in her hair, as did Fiona and Naomi, who now cavorted among the guests in the round chapel in the redwoods, the bright afternoon sun filtering through the trees. Their lavender chiffon dresses mirrored Rebecca's dark purple one. The group sauntered to the building next door and gathered in a loose circle. Kate and Mike joined Ellen and her date; Mark and his girlfriend; Jeffrey and Ben with their dates; Brad; and next to him, Martha and Greg.

Ellen sidled up to Kate, who held Hannah. "So, how'd you convince your mom to come?"

Kate gave Ellen a sly look. "I suggested to Fiona and Naomi that they invite her. Who can resist them, especially as flower girls?"

Ellen cackled as Kate crossed the room and gave Hannah

back to Rebecca, who nuzzled and kissed her baby, reveling in her warmth. It had been a whole hour since she had held her. She needed a moment. But, too soon, someone handed Reuben and Rebecca glasses of champagne. Rebecca leaned against Reuben, holding their baby between them, champagne in her other hand.

Mark and Ellen stood in the center of the circle and raised their glasses. Everyone quieted and raised theirs. "To Rebecca and Reuben," Mark said, and Ellen added, "To a lifetime of happiness together." Everyone cheered and clinked glasses. Rebecca waited until conversations resumed over appetizers before slipping away to nurse Hannah.

*   *   *

Martha sank into a large armchair in the far corner of the reception room as the festivities continued. It had been an exhausting day. Celebration bubbled all around her, but she didn't feel joyous; she felt conspicuous. What had she expected? Why had she come? Well, the answer to this wasn't easy; couldn't anyone tell that? Would she rather have stayed home? Would she rather she hadn't been invited? She guessed it meant something that Rebecca invited her. Maybe Greg was right. Maybe Rebecca has changed. At least she did the right thing and got married.

"May I join you?" Brad's voice from behind startled her.

"Sure," Martha said, though she felt guarded. He had

pushed her to come to this, and she might have resisted altogether if Naomi and Fiona hadn't charmed her into it.

He handed her a fresh glass of champagne. "It was a great wedding, wasn't it?" Brad said smiling as he sat. "They seem really happy."

She held her glass without drinking. "I guess."

"And how can you resist Hannah? When Kate's kids were born, you couldn't stop cuddling them and playing with them. How come you're staying away now?"

"I'm … I'm just feeling cautious, Brad. I'm just not sure that Rebecca wants me that close."

"She invited you here today, didn't she? I'd say that's a pretty good indication."

"Yes, she invited me. But she hasn't exactly gone out of her way to be what you could call friendly."

Brad looked incredulous. "*She* hasn't been friendly? What about you? Don't you think she has as much reason to be cautious as you do?"

Martha stayed quiet for a minute. "It's been hard," she finally said.

"Yes, it has." Brad took a sip of champagne. "Anyway," he said, changing his tone, "Hannah's adorable. You have to admit that."

Martha didn't reply. *Of course Hannah's "adorable,"* she thought. *But she has Rebecca's eyes. It's uncanny. She looks exactly like Rebecca did at that age. Like she did all through our childhood. Can't he see that? Or maybe he does see it, but that's not a problem for him.* She sighed. "I don't know how to explain it to you, Brad."

"Try me."

"Hannah reminds me too much of …."

"Of Rebecca?"

She nodded.

"Well, there *is* this quirky thing called genetics that sometimes rears its ugly head."

"I don't need sarcasm, Brad. I just need to figure this out on my own, okay?"

Brad shrugged and stood. "Okay." He kissed Martha on her head, squeezed her shoulder, and walked back to the reception room.

From her chair, Martha could watch Fiona and Naomi outside, chasing each other across the lawn and around the trees. Now they ran to Rebecca's friend, Ellen, as she came out of the chapel carrying the large floral arrangement toward the reception area. They followed her inside, where she set it on a table, pulled out several flowers from the outer edges of the arrangement, and gave them to the girls. Then they spotted Martha and ran to show her their flowers.

"Ohh, aren't these beautiful?" Martha exclaimed as the girls piled the flowers in her lap. "Let's look at each of them." They sniffed one flower at a time and exclaimed over the different petal shapes and hues. Then she said, "Let's divide them up so you each have the same amount in your bouquets." They watched her carefully while she did this. "An iris for Fiona, an iris for Naomi. A daisy for Fiona, a daisy for Naomi." She continued until all of the flowers were divided equally. Fortunately, Martha thought, they started with an even number. "There. Now it's just right," she said. The girls gathered up their bouquets, squeezed into the large armchair with Martha, and settled in, fingering the blossoms and smelling them while Martha stroked her granddaughters' hair.

*　　　　　*　　　　　*

Reuben came into the bathroom with a fluffy towel straight out of the dryer, as Rebecca pulled Hannah out of the bath. He wrapped the towel around Hannah, bundling her in it and taking her from Rebecca. Hannah smiled, but her eyelids were already beginning to droop. It had been a big day with lots of activity, and she had been passed around and cooed at by more people than she was used to. It was a lot to handle for a one-month-old. Reuben and Rebecca took her to bed and lay on either side of her.

"She's almost asleep already," Rebecca smiled as she rubbed her baby's tummy.

"I am, too," Reuben smiled with a yawn. "I'm glad we're staying home for our honeymoon."

She smiled. "Me too."

Hannah made soft gurgling sounds, opening and closing her eyes lazily. Opening them again, she looked more steadily at Rebecca.

"Aww," Rebecca whispered to her. "You still want a song?"

Reuben chuckled. "She's addicted to your voice."

"Okay, sweetheart," Rebecca whispered to Hannah. "Good night, my Dear One." And she began to sing.

Goodnight, my dear one, your quilt awaits
To wrap you warm, and bless your dreams
Pillows tenderly cradle you
Sink soft in your bed, safe and loved

Reuben watched Rebecca. When she sang to Hannah, she always seemed to be in a different world—so immersed, focusing on her child. She sang many different songs to Hannah, but this one appeared most often in her repertoire. He had once asked her where she learned it.

"I don't really know," Rebecca had said, slightly puzzled, but not concerned. "I don't think I knew it when I was a child. It just started running through my head after I got pregnant. I have no idea where I heard it."

Reuben listened to more.

Stars beckon you to join their dance
In the Milky Way sky above
Enchanted in celestial ballet
They smile on you, beautiful child

Reuben loved that part.

Now with you here, the world is kinder
My heart overflows with love for you

He watched her as she kissed Hannah's cheek.

Your light shines bright upon us all
My life's treasure, my greatest joy

What a different life Rebecca was living now. He loved to watch how she savored it.

> My love surrounds you, near and far
> Love surrounds you, now and always
> When you awake and venture forth
> My love will surround you still

Hannah was deep into sleep before the song ended. Her parents were not far behind.

*   *   *

Martha slung the last of the plates into the dishwasher and slammed the door shut. "I cannot *believe* that you invited them!" she raged. "For Christmas, of all times!" She began to wipe down the counters with a vengeance.

Greg stood on the other side of the kitchen island. "They invited us to their wedding. It seemed like the next step. The words just popped right out."

"Hah!" Martha ran the rag under the faucet and wrung it out tightly, then shook it open.

Greg took a deep breath and squared his shoulders. "I thought it was about time we invited them back into our family activities." He spoke quietly, but an edge was creeping into his voice. "Besides, you seemed to be comfortable enough at the wedding. I thought things had gotten better."

"Well, I *survived* it just fine, but Greg? It was *stressful*. How could you not realize that? And we're talking about *Christmas*! This is different! Christmas is *my* time with *my* children and *my* grandchildren! How could you do this?" Her voice cracked with frustration.

Greg planted his hands on the island. "You are not the only person in this house. Kate is my daughter, too. Naomi and Fiona are my granddaughters, too."

She threw the rag into the sink and turned to face him. "You—"

"*And* Hannah is my niece, too," he interrupted, his voice gaining volume. "Rebecca and Reuben are fully committed parents. What do you have against that? And now they're married, too. You've always acted like *that* was the problem. Now the 'problem' has been addressed. What more do you want from them?"

"How can I relax with *them* here? And that's a whole lot more food to cook, and I'll have to clean, and—"

"Oh, please, Martha, you clean anyway. You cook anyway."

"Just my point! Where are *you* when I'm doing all that? You're never around to help. It's all on me while you go out on your boat and ...."

"And what?"

"You're never home! You leave it all up to me!" Martha leaned her back against the counter and rubbed her forehead in silence for a moment. "You should have talked it over with me," she said, her voice heavy with defeat and resentment.

Greg's shoulders dropped. "Yes. I should have." He stared at empty air for a moment. "Yes. I should have," he repeated.

"But even if I had, what difference would it have made? You would have refused. But," he hesitated. "Yes. I should have talked it over with you. I apologize for not doing that. It *is* your Christmas, too. But you seem to forget that it is also *my* Christmas. Not just yours."

Now Martha rubbed her forehead with both hands. "I don't know why Christmas is suddenly important to you, anyway," she spit out. "You never cared about it before. You've always stayed on the sidelines, like you couldn't wait to get out of the house. You're never home anymore; you act like you can barely tolerate being here. Now suddenly it's Christmas, and you want to stage a family reunion?"

Greg crossed his arms and stayed quiet for a moment. Then, letting both arms open wide in surrender, he burst out, "Martha, I can't do this anymore."

At his change in tone, Martha jerked her eyes directly toward him. Her voice quavered. "What does that mean?"

"I can't keep having power struggles with you."

"*Power* struggles?" Martha threw her hands up. "Since when did you ever *not* get your way?" she shrieked. "When have I ever prevented you from going out without me, leaving me here to do everything?"

"Martha, we have not been happy for years. You know this. We have different priorities, different views, different personalities. We argue, but we never resolve anything. We keep stuffing our real feelings to keep the peace. What for? Our daughter is grown and doing well. Why do we keep going through a show of togetherness when we are anything but? Sometimes I think that you hate Rebecca and Reuben because they had the guts *years ago* to leave marriages that they were unhappy in, and we didn't. What else did they do that was so wrong? Ted's not unhappy anymore. Cathy isn't unhappy anymore. They've moved on, they've forgiven Reuben and Rebecca, and *they* are happy. But *you* continue to be unhappy. What does that tell you?"

"Why are you suddenly all chummy with Reuben and Rebecca? Where did that come from? Why are you taking her side?"

"I'm not *suddenly chummy*. I'm just tired of this hypocrisy, this charade. I thought … I don't know, I guess it was a stupid impulse." He tried again. "I thought that inviting them might, I don't know … change the tone around here." He shrugged and shook his head.

Martha glowered at him, then turned away. "I can't talk about this anymore. I'm taking a walk." She grabbed a sweater from the coat hook and stalked out, slamming the door behind her. It ricocheted away from the metal jamb and opened again. Greg still hadn't fixed that damn door. He used to be obsessive about repairs. Now *everything* waited for her. She cursed and stomped back. She turned the knob with deliberation and yanked the door shut as loudly as she could.

*   *   *

Greg stood in the kitchen, leaning on the center island,

and stared ahead. He wasn't kidding. He really didn't want to do this anymore. He scanned the kitchen, pausing at every corner, every cupboard, yet not actually seeing them so much as considering something not in the room. He took a deep breath, held it for a moment, then blew it out. Then, finally deciding, he pulled his phone from his pocket.

"Hi, it's me. Are you home right now? I need to see you. Okay; I'll be right there."

He turned off his phone and walked out the door, carefully turning the knob all the way and letting the door click firmly behind him.

*   *   *

Brad put his coffee mug down on the end table and watched Hannah snoozing in Rebecca's arms.

"So," he said. "You got invited to Greg and Martha's for Christmas?"

"Well, *Greg* invited us," Rebecca said. "I wonder how on-board Martha really is about it. We usually spend Christmas with Jeffrey and Ben. It's always nice and peaceful. We're not sure we're up to dealing with whatever stress could come along with visiting Martha, so we're most likely going to stick with our usual plan."

"She could surprise you," Brad shrugged. "At least she came to the wedding. That was a huge step for her."

"True," Rebecca conceded. Then she peered carefully at

him. "Did you have anything to do with that?" she asked him.

"Well, I did talk to her," he said. "But I'm sure Naomi and Fiona's charms are what sealed the deal." He sipped more coffee and looked thoughtful. "I don't really have a right to give advice about any of this, do I," he reflected, "since my strategy for dealing with her—and our parents before that— was to stay three thousand miles away. I'm impressed with you for inviting her to the wedding. That was a gutsy thing to do. And, these days I'm feeling guilty for hardly ever coming out of my hiding place in Vermont, and, well, I guess I want to do *something*. I hate to see this misery you are both feeling. I was a crappy big brother to you both. I ran away the second I got out of high school. Even when I was here, I buried myself in sports and anything I could find, just to stay out of the house. I wasn't there for either of you. I've been going to therapy the last couple of years, and I … well, I feel bad, and I want to see if there's anything I can do to help. A bit late, now, I know. I'm sorry." He reached over to Rebecca's shoulder. She scooted over and hugged him, with Hannah in the middle. Hannah started to fuss, so Rebecca eased back and rocked her.

Brad continued, "But you do have an invitation for Christmas now, so maybe there is a chink in her armor. And at least at a big family gathering with everyone, you'll be a bit insulated. Plus, she'll be so caught up with her granddaughters and putting on her stylish dinner, she'll barely notice that you're there. Maybe with a little more time she'll see that you are really not so bad after all."

Rebecca said nothing.

"Scruff, you know it's not about *you*. And it's not about

Reuben, or your relationship. Becca, you have to know that. It's just who she is. Maybe she needs some compassion."

"I tried that," Rebecca said flatly. "And what about me? What the hell did I ever do to her?"

"You were in the wrong place at the wrong time," Brad said sadly.

*   *   *

Martha pulled her sweater more tightly around herself. In her rush to get out of the house, she'd forgotten how chilly it was outside. Her agitation mounted. *I should have grabbed my jacket instead of this flimsy thing.*

She walked briskly to the corner, turned left, and continued without slowing. *Greg is unhappy with the marriage? Well, I've got news for you buddy; I'm not exactly thrilled with things myself. Why should I be? You're never home, you never take me seriously, you never ....*

Martha stopped short. *Where does he go all the time? He has barely touched me in ... how long? He never talks with me about his day anymore. It's like he doesn't care if I'm in his life, and now he's getting obsessed with his car. He never did that before. Now he's waxing it, vacuuming it out. What's that about? And he's preening in the mirror like never before, too. Like he's ....*

No, no.

She walked faster, planting each step firmly on the sidewalk, walking through grass clippings that Mr. Fenton had left yesterday. He never swept after mowing. She realized that, if she was outside his house, she was already almost completely around her block. She looked at her own house; she felt as if it were somehow mocking her. She focused on the sidewalk again and kept going. She couldn't go back inside yet.

*   *   *

Rebecca answered her phone.

"Becca? It's Kate."

"Hi, Katie."

"Um … so … you got an invitation for Christmas?"

"Yes, but we're still thinking about it. And to be honest, I'm not so sure I'm up for it, especially since I'm wondering if your mom might not have had anything to do with the invitation. I don't want to push things."

"Well, I'm calling to tell you that it's off. I mean, not just your invitation. Mom isn't going to do the Christmas thing now."

"What?"

"Dad left her. He got his own apartment and everything."

"What?" Rebecca said again.

"I know. I can't really wrap my brain around this."

"This is wild."

"Becca, he's …." Kate began.

Rebecca waited.

Kate tried again. "There's another woman."

*   *   *

January

Rebecca mailed the signed papers that extended her leave of absence until June. Only two months had passed since Hannah's birth. Being up half the night with her took its toll. A day or two of sleeplessness she could handle with reasonable humor and good nature, but after five nights in a row of being awake more of the night than she slept, she knew she would lose her train of thought and make no sense during lessons or student dramas, and certainly would not keep up with the paperwork. These realities made her decision easier.

Besides, Rebecca savored her time with Hannah more than she had dreamed possible. Right now, she couldn't imagine leaving her. She reveled in their time together, and whenever Hannah *did* sleep peacefully (mostly during daylight hours), even though she could have slept then too, Rebecca found herself just watching her, watching her, unable to tear herself away to do the chores she thought she would finally do when her hands were free. Sure, she was tired. But life had never been better.

And she loved watching Reuben be a daddy to Hannah. He talked to her tenderly, just as he had when she was in the womb. He changed her and walked the floor with her so that Rebecca could have a break, but of course, ultimately, it was

Rebecca who fed her; she lost the most sleep, the most free time. Once in a while, she felt chained down, but even so, she felt a deep joy when Hannah was at her breast. She felt calmer and more grounded than she had ever felt in her life.

Two Years Later

January

Two-year-old Hannah arranged her menagerie of stuffed animals on the couch. Clutching her library book in one hand, she hoisted herself onto the ottoman, scooting her seat with a twist one way, then another, until she found her just-right position. She opened the book and began to read, using the same characters in the story, but sometimes with her own variations of events, some words understandable to others, some only to herself. Either way, her inflection echoed that of Gilda, the children's librarian, who had read to her toddler group that morning. At the end of each page, Hannah turned the book around and, with an unsteady horizontal arc, showed the pictures to her rapt audience.

Rebecca and Ellen watched, amused, from the kitchen table. "I can't get over how well she mimics Gilda," Rebecca remarked, shaking her head. "She's crazy about story time at the library. It's good for her to be with the other kids, too. Oh!

And I have to tell you this. A while back, we checked out an animated video about some elves that live in a forest. And now, whenever we're in the garden, she looks behind leaves and says, "Elfs? Elfs?"

"Aww," Ellen smiled. "How are things going with your babysitting exchange with Kate?"

"It's been great. Hannah loves to follow Naomi and Fiona around, no matter what they're doing, and they have fun indulging her."

"How old are Naomi and Fiona now?" Ellen asked.

"Six and four! Can you believe it? Lately they've all been enjoying Kate's trunk of dress-up clothes. Hannah especially loves the hats; I suppose because they are easier for her to put on and remove than the clothes are."

"Has Martha joined in with the babysitting yet?"

"No, she always manages to have some other commitment on the days Kate takes Hannah."

Ellen rolled her eyes. "Funny how that works out."

"Yes, but, in all fairness, Kate says that Martha and Greg have been on again-off again for a couple of years now, and I'm sure that has a lot to do with it. Martha has taken him back a couple of times, and then he bails on her again when he finds someone else. That's got to be hard. I never would have expected Greg to do that, but there it is. Kate says it feels to her like this last split is the last time, though. It sounds like Martha is getting stronger and more realistic."

"Wow. Mr. and Mrs. Stability break out of the mold," Ellen quipped.

"Hm." Rebecca shrugged. "Meanwhile, I'm fine with her

not getting involved in Hannah's life, because, sheesh! I don't want her there if she resents it or has any other bad feelings. That wouldn't be good for Hannah. I just feel bad about the spot that puts Kate in, having to juggle her schedule so much. Not only to divide her attention equally between her parents now, but around her mom's issues about me and Hannah. Often that comes down to Naomi and Fiona getting less time with Martha, which isn't fair to anyone."

"No, it's not," Ellen agreed. "Do you think she'll ever come around?"

"I don't know. But I can't worry about it. It's funny how it doesn't feel like as big of a deal as it could, because, well, my life is so full of Hannah. My heart feels more content now than I ever thought possible, so that leaves less room for angst, I guess."

Ellen looked at Rebecca for a long minute. "You know, it used to be I wouldn't believe you when you said things like that. But now ...." She gave her lifelong friend a satisfied smile. "Now I believe you."

February

Reuben and Rebecca strolled down the sidewalk. It was a mild evening, and, after a delicious dinner in their favorite seafood restaurant, they walked hand in hand, delaying their return home. Ann had pushed them to start having date nights as early as possible. Rebecca had resisted at first, finding it impossible to leave Hannah, but now she was glad that Ann had kept nagging her about it. It gave her perspective to get out into the world again. And she and Reuben needed time to talk to each other—to actually *see* each other—without distraction, even if they did talk about Hannah most of the time. Hannah was two years and three months old now. These date nights had been a habit for almost two years. It should have been easy to leave her after all this time, but Rebecca kept checking her phone compulsively, even though she knew Hannah was in good hands with Kate and Mike.

Soft Spanish guitar notes drifted to them through the mild evening air, luring them to a rustic coffee bar with its door propped open. They entered, ordered decaf cappuccinos with cinnamon, and took the last seats in the back, in a cozy corner lined with art posters. Rebecca loved this kind of guitar music. She held Reuben's hand and let her mind drift, feeling like she was young again, with nowhere to be and no one to look after.

But after a few more songs, reality set in and she realized how tired she was. Chasing a two-year-old around took its toll. She nudged Reuben, and he recognized her expression. He swigged the rest of his cappuccino, catching that extra sludge of cinnamon that he especially liked, before they tiptoed out.

Arms around each other's waists, they meandered to the car, stretching out their freedom for as long as they could, in spite of their fatigue. They took the scenic route home on the two-lane wooded road alongside the reservoir, still holding hands.

When another car approached from the opposite way, Reuben flipped his high beams to low. The other driver didn't do the same. In fact, the lights became brighter and brighter, and the angle didn't seem right to Reuben. He let go of Rebecca's hand, flashed his lights again at the other driver, and honked his horn, but there was no more time. He swerved sharply to the right.

*   *   *

Kate approached the counter, trembling.

"May I help you?" the woman asked.

"Someone called me and told me to ask for Officer Fallini? Or something like that. I'm not sure if I got it right."

"Your name?"

"Kate Mallory."

"Officer Fiorini," the woman nodded. "I'll call him for you." She picked up the phone.

Kate paced the mottled green tile, feeling nauseated, disoriented. She jumped when a man's voice called her name.

*   *   *

Kate couldn't drive herself home. She called Mike, but her voice failed her. He figured out enough, and promised her that he would call right back with a plan.

He got on the phone with Lorraine next door, who came to

stay with Naomi, Fiona, and Hannah, while he headed for the funeral home.

*　　　　　*　　　　　*

According to Officer Fiorini, the other driver was texting, which phone records verified. "The driver has told us little, mostly insisting on his right to remain silent," the officer said, "but what we're positing for the moment is that when he came around that last curve, he looked up just in time to see another car plummet over the edge. After it was too late, he swerved back into his lane, overcompensated, and plowed into some bushes. Minor damages to him and his car, but it was enough to keep him at the scene. We're still investigating for more details."

Reuben's car was a 1963 Corvette. He had installed seatbelts, but it was not possible to add airbags. He and Rebecca had bought a safe family car to use with Hannah, but he couldn't resist keeping his old classic, and they enjoyed using it on dates.

What had first appeared to be a mild slope on the right side of the road turned out to be much steeper than Reuben had been able to see in the dark after being blinded by the other driver's high beams. After pitching over the edge, the car rolled, flipped, and landed upside-down as it slammed head-on into a large tree trunk. The front of the car compressed immediately; the motor slammed into Rebecca and the steering wheel crushed Reuben. They both died instantly.

*   *   *

Kate sat at the table in the small conference room with the officer. She rested her head in her arms on the table, afraid that she would pass out. The woman at the counter brought her a cup of water and stood with her hand on Kate's shoulder. She told Kate that Jeffrey and Ben were on their way. Kate wanted to see them, wanted them to say, *Oh, no, of course this is not real; Dad and Rebecca are still in the restaurant.* But she had seen Rebecca's body. The officer told her she didn't have to look; the ID was sufficient. She just needed to sign some papers. But she had to. She needed to know if it was really true. But she didn't want to know. And she looked at Reuben, too. She had to know. She had vomited on the floor. The officer was very kind to her, brought moist paper towels for her to wipe her mouth. It felt surreal to do something as mundane as wipe her mouth. She had to get out of there. But she didn't want to leave until she saw Jeffrey and Ben. They would tell her it was a mistake. But no, it wasn't. No. She wouldn't be able to bear seeing them. She would know from their faces that it was true. And she had to see Hannah. She had to hold her girls. She couldn't have Jeffrey and Ben make it real. She had to go.

Mike pulled into their garage. He got out, went around, and helped Kate out of the car. With his arm firmly around her waist, she leaned on him all the way inside the house, feeling that her knees would buckle any moment, that she would never be able to walk again. Thankfully, Lorraine had read extra stories to Naomi and Fiona and they were sleeping now. Lorraine would stay as long as needed. With Mike helping her, Kate checked on her girls, then staggered into the room where Hannah slept. She picked her up and sank into the rocker. She held Hannah, warm with sleep, to her chest. Now, finally, now, the tears broke through every seam of her being. She rocked Hannah and wept. She squeezed her closer and wept. She petted her soft curls and kissed her head. And wept. And wept. And wept.

Part Two

Rebecca felt cozier and more relaxed than she'd felt in ages. Lying on her side, a soft mattress and pillow cradled her legs, hips, torso, neck and head just right. Silky-smooth cotton sheets and a lightweight quilted comforter lay over her, stopping just below her chin.

It must be Saturday morning. No school! She realized it might even be the first day of summer vacation, because she could hear a slight vibrato in the elongated sigh of a manual lawnmower; the warm breeze carried the smell of freshly cut grass to her nostrils.

Ahh. Certainly the first day of summer. Fourth grade had been a great year. And now it was time to goof off.

She stretched, contented, her eyes closed, as she rolled onto her back, extending her arms above her head with a long luxurious yawn.

Aware of her stretch, she became more alert. Her eyebrows furrowed at the sensation of her legs and arms. They were longer than they had been when she was ten.

Her mind suddenly cleared a bit more, like a projection on a screen popping into focus. Her eyes opened. "I am a grown woman!" she realized. She sat up.

The lovely cut-grass aroma continued, along with the soft mower sigh, and a *chick-a-dee-dee-dee!* dialogue between two birds. But now the earthy scent of coffee came to her. She surveyed her feet, her hands. Yes. A grown woman, even though she felt remarkably supple and energetic. Every joint seemed happy to move as she climbed out of bed. Every limb felt lighter than it ever had in her fifty-two years.

She explored the room. It was the garret room she

had always dreamed of as a girl. Slanted white ceilings met white walls; blue gingham curtains framed two large dormer windows; a patchwork quilt graced her bed; squishy pillows of green, purple, and red were strewn casually on the bed and on a large wicker chair. Her favorite mysteries, fairy tales, and nature books filled an entire wall of bookshelves. Rocks and shells were arranged in front of the books. The open windows welcomed the summer morning breeze into the room. She leaned out one of the windows, resting her elbows on the sill. From her second-story view, she could see a lawn, freshly mowed, with a sprinkler set in the middle, and a little girl in shorts and a tank top doing barefooted cartwheels through the spray.

"Whee-hoo!" the girl squealed. "Haa-hoo!"

Rebecca smiled at the scene. She felt a tug of remembered delight at doing the same thing long ago. She turned to go downstairs and outside, then found herself already at the edge of the lawn. It felt odd to her that she had no memory of walking through the house or out the door, but she had already begun to feel that this was a dream, and dreams have a way of instantly shifting scenes, so she noted it without concern.

The little girl, with strawberry blonde pigtails, finished one more cartwheel. She flashed a delighted smile at Rebecca, and walked quickly toward her. "Rebecca," she said. "My dear one, I'm so happy to see you." Smile lines appeared around her vivid blue eyes. And Rebecca saw before her a tall elderly lady, not a little girl. The woman had white hair pulled gently into a bun, and now wore a cotton short-sleeved dress with a small floral print. She was still barefoot, however.

"Lydia?" Rebecca gasped. She burst into a smile and threw

her arms around the old woman. Lydia returned her hug with more gusto than Rebecca remembered her old neighbor ever having. Rebecca's feeling of puzzlement grew. She released Lydia and looked again.

"Isn't it fun?" Lydia's eyes sparkled. "I could do the cartwheels as I am now." She demonstrated with three across the lawn and three back again, as her dress fluttered. "But I get a real kick out of having a six-year-old body again."

Rebecca smiled with pleasure at seeing her friend's antics, and noticed that, oddly, she did not feel her usual need to explain how any of this could be possible.

Rebecca had first met Lydia when she was two years old and had wandered out of her Berkeley backyard through an open gate to the yard next door. Her mother, inside on the phone, hadn't noticed. Rebecca found Lydia digging in her garden, unaware yet of her visitor. Two-year-old Rebecca had stared in wonderment around Lydia's yard with so many glorious flowers. She was about to explore further when Lydia turned over the moist soil with her trowel, revealing a squiggly earthworm. With a delighted "Oooh!" Rebecca had toddled over. Lydia, only mildly surprised to see Rebecca, let her scoop the pile of damp soil with both hands (which Rebecca's mother would *never* have allowed) to inspect the worm. And with that smudgy wide-eyed exploration, their friendship began.

Over the years, with tensions at home rising, Lydia's house became Rebecca's retreat after school and on weekends. She often did her homework at Lydia's kitchen table, or—on nice days—at the wooden picnic table in the backyard that sat under a redwood tree. Rebecca let Lydia read the stories she had written while she ate Lydia's homemade cookies. Together, they hunted for bugs in the yard, and looked up every one they found. Later, she encouraged Rebecca as she explored colleges, telling her that she should go wherever they would recognize and nurture "that wonderful brain" of hers. Rebecca found it hard to decide where to go, since she didn't want to move far from her friend. But one day in eleventh grade, Rebecca came home to learn that Lydia had collapsed in the grocery store from a heart attack and died. Her grown children sold the house, and Rebecca felt lost.

Tears welled in her eyes as Rebecca remembered the pain of losing her friend. "I've missed you so much!" she whispered.

Lydia reached out and placed her hand on Rebecca's heart. Instantly, Rebecca felt that old anxious pain of loss replaced with calm. She felt her spirits lift, though she hardly knew why.

"We're together now, my dear. All is well." Lydia said gently, with a wide smile.

Rebecca felt better. But she also became more alert. "Wait. What is going on? Lydia, is this a dream?"

Lydia wiped her hands on her dress, just the way she used to on her work clothes when she was done weeding and it was time to go in. (Even though Lydia had not been weeding now, Rebecca thought, and she smiled, remembering that Lydia always had used this gesture more for subject changes than anything else.) "Okay, I need to get you up to date. Are you ready for a nice cup of coffee?"

Rebecca remembered the fresh coffee that she'd smelled earlier, and craved it now. She put her questions aside for the moment. "Yes! I'd love some."

Lydia led her to a wooden gazebo. On a round oak table were two smooth earthen mugs that had been Rebecca's favorite in Lydia's kitchen, a matching coffee pot, a cream pitcher, and a plate full of oatmeal chocolate chip cookies.

They sat and Lydia poured the coffee. "There's cream, and sugar too, if you'd like. You can have anything you want here, and you'll stay as healthy as can be. That goes for cookies too," she winked.

Rebecca smiled at her friend and put two cookies on her plate. Lydia grabbed a handful.

"The first thing you need to know, dear, is that there is plenty of time and all is well. Do you understand what I am saying?"

Rebecca nodded, even though she was not at all sure where Lydia was going with this. The warmth and pleasure she'd noticed earlier continued to envelope her like a soft blanket. She took a bite from her first cookie. Lydia's voice continued, but her words were upstaged by the flavors in Rebecca's mouth. She inspected the cookie up close, took another bite, and closed her eyes. She chewed more slowly. The freshest walnuts, dark chocolate chips, oats, and a touch of cinnamon and nutmeg exploded together into a chorus of flavors. Her shoulders sagged as she let out a loud "Mmmm." Certainly, it was delicious. But that wasn't it. There was something else she couldn't place, something marvelous that went beyond her ordinary senses.

She opened her eyes and looked once more at the cookie, then at Lydia, who had stopped talking.

Lydia was grinning at her. "Yes, I know. I've got to learn

to stop talking when someone tries these cookies for the first time." She took another bite of her own, and the two women let the flavors roll over their tongues for a few moments.

"Mmmm," Lydia nodded with satisfaction before she continued. "Okay. Now, I'll be explaining all kinds of things to you for a while. It might seem like a lot, but don't worry. You'll absorb it without effort, and you'll remember any of it whenever the need arises. It will give you more clarity and confidence before you move forward."

Rebecca took another bite of cookie. She felt confused, but strangely at ease. This was not a normal reaction for her. Usually when she wanted to learn something new, she felt energized and impatient. But now, all she could think to ask was, "What do you mean, 'move forward'?"

"You have something that you want to do. It's out of your focus for the moment. It'll become clear soon enough. Just remember that there is plenty of time. I need you to trust me and repeat this: there is plenty of time, and all is well."

"Okay. There is plenty of time. And all is well."

"Good girl. Let's get started." Lydia popped the last chunk of cookie into her mouth and finished it. "The first thing," she continued, "is that you might not remember, but you've actually had many experiences since you've arrived. However, at this stage, you can only remember one thing at a time. This is to make things as easy as possible for you. After a while, you'll remember one, then another, and later another. Eventually you'll be able to remember them all at once, and it will feel completely manageable."

"You know it's funny you say that," Rebecca said, "Because

just now, while you poured the coffee, I kept having a sense of another experience besides sitting at this table. It feels like a dream I might have had right before I woke up this morning."

"Yes," Lydia smiled at her friend. "Tell me the dream."

"Well ...." Rebecca felt just like she was back in Lydia's kitchen in high school, telling her about what she had dreamed. They used to talk about what their dreams might mean. Lydia had studied Carl Jung and learned that a good way to remember more detail about a dream is to tell it in the present tense. So Rebecca began in this way.

"I wake up snuggled in a cozy cotton quilt. I'm warm, but not too warm—just right, and I feel completely safe. The lighting is soft and subtle, but I have the sense of all colors—blue, violet, red; all the colors in the rainbow. And there is this energy, almost like someone humming, that is, well, joyous. And I gradually become aware that someone is, well, it's as if they are lightly brushing their fingers along my face, my shoulders, and with every brushing movement, I feel like something—no, not just one thing, like many strands of something ... I think. Pain, fear, tension ... are being gently pulled out of every joint in my body, every muscle, down to my feet—and the tensions get pulled right out, like strands that connected all the way to my head. I don't think I was fully aware that all those kinds of pain were there until they are removed. It's not like *all* pain is removed, but a lot of ... something recent. I'm not sure about that. Anyway, I feel better—and lighter. Like there's less gravity, physical *and* emotional gravity. Hmm. I didn't think of that 'til just now. And I feel peaceful, strong, and healthy. And ... loved, in a way I never knew possible, and my muscles feel like they've had a wonderfully deep massage. And then I feel myself sinking into a lovelier rest than I've ever felt from any good night's sleep. After that, I wake up in that cozy bed, feeling ten years old! And then I see you out the window." Rebecca gave her friend a puzzled smile.

Lydia smiled back at Rebecca. "You'll experience that again at other times," she said. "Because even though fear and a great deal of pain has been lifted from you, there are a few more layers that will be taken in stages. It is easier for us to perceive if it happens that way, rather than suddenly. But I can see that you are about to remember something that happened before then. So I need to remind you of these statements again. Please indulge me, sweetheart, and repeat after me: there is plenty of time."

Rebecca responded with trust in her friend. "There is plenty of time."

"All is well."

"All is well," Rebecca repeated.

"And now this one: whatever we do here, whatever we talk about, however long it takes, it is the same as a *millisecond* on the earthly plane."

"Whatever we do here, whatever we talk about, however long it takes ...." Rebecca hesitated.

"It is the same as a millisecond on the earthly plane," Lydia finished.

"It is the same as a millisecond ...." Rebecca felt a swirl of colors in her brain. "On the ...." *Wait. Something's happening.* "On the *earthly plane*?" Rebecca felt as if everything around her was swirling. Something familiar felt far away. Faces she knew, but they're not here right now. A face she knows and loves that is right here but hasn't seen since....

Rebecca stood up and stared at Lydia.

"You died!" she gasped at Lydia. "But you're here! You can do cartwheels! I *am* dreaming! No, that's not it." Rebecca rubbed her forehead. "What is this place? How did I get here? Wait." Traveling into colors and light, supporting arms, serenity and healing … from …. Careening. Loud crashing.

"Hannah! Reuben!" Rebecca lurched away from the table and looked in every direction. Under normal circumstances, she would be panicked. But right now, though disoriented, she was not exactly scared. This confused her even more. She found Lydia next to her, a firm arm around her shoulders, guiding her to an overstuffed couch in the middle of her old flower garden. Rebecca sat gratefully, leaning against Lydia.

Lydia spoke softly to her. "You're remembering."

Rebecca nodded silently, trying to catch her breath. She could remember it all now. Hannah's sweet smell, cuddling, kissing her good-bye, laughing with Reuben, walking arm in arm, the car, the headlights, the touch of Reuben's hand, diving into a dark tunnel, strange dimensions.

"Wait … Reuben …. Where's Reuben? Did he survive the crash?"

"No, dear. He's here, too. You'll see him soon. But everyone always starts here separately, with their own guide. People get more clarity that way. If you immediately focused on someone who *also* just arrived, you would be more likely to stay in your previous frame of mind, and it would be harder to heal and see the possibilities that lie before you."

"Hannah ...." Rebecca felt her heart open and a strange lost-searching sensation. How she ached for her baby!

Lydia held Rebecca closer. "This is where it helps to remember that however long we take here, it is the same as a millisecond to those we've left behind. Which means that right now, Hannah is snoozing at Kate and Mike's. Kate hasn't even gotten the phone call yet. All is well."

Rebecca sat up and looked into Lydia's eyes. "They don't know yet?"

"Not yet. By the time they do, you will have found your bearings a bit more, and will better understand what you can do. I know this is hard to believe right now, but it will be okay."

And now Rebecca knew that this was true. She sank back into the cushions of the couch and leaned against Lydia. She felt grateful for the security of her friend's familiar arm around her once again, as she began to settle a bit into what she had just figured out.

"It's weird, Lydia. I mean, I'm really glad to see you again. But I never really pictured, well ...." Rebecca trailed off, not sure of what she meant.

"If you thought of heaven at all, you probably wouldn't have pictured me greeting you?"

"Right! Um, no offense," she put her hand on Lydia's arm.

Lydia laughed. "None taken. It's not like I was the most spiritual person you ever met." She smiled, kissed Rebecca's head and hugged her closer. Rebecca could smell traces of cookie breath. "It's because this is so strange to all of us when we first get here. Everyone has preconceived notions, and we all end up feeling a bit thrown for a loop. So, to start off, we always get greeted by someone we already know and trust. After a while, you'll mingle with lots of other people. Some you knew before, and some you'll meet for the first time. But to start, it helps to feel safe and loved in a familiar way first."

Rebecca looked up to see her old friend smiling like she was remembering something wonderful.

"For me," Lydia reminisced, "I was greeted by my big brother, Charles, who took care of me from the time he was a teenager and I was quite young, when our father was off to war and our mother had to work long hours at the factory. I think I've told you about him. He died many years before I did."

"Yes, I remember."

"There I was one day, choosing cantaloupes at the grocery store, and the next thing I knew, I saw Charles with his arms open, right in front of me! He swung me up to ride on his shoulders, just like he had when I was little!" She laughed happily.

Rebecca watched her friend for a minute, then began to puzzle out a new question. "Okay, wait. I died. I'm *here*. We're having cookies. I'm walking around. You're doing cartwheels. But our bodies ...." She flexed her hands trying to fathom this mystery. "How can we have bodies? After what happened? Have we been healed? Or ...." Rebecca paused and shook her head, trying to shake loose a new idea. She looked to her mentor for help.

"We're given the *sensation* of a body, just as a point of reference," Lydia explained. "It helps avoid confusion. They tell me that when we've been here a while, and after we've learned a lot more, we won't need that sensation any more, and we move on. I'm not ready for that change yet, myself. It happens gradually. I see some people in the process of it, and I notice extra glints of colored light coming from them here and there, sometimes even in their eyes. But, like everything else here, it's different for everyone. At any rate, for now, this sensation of still being physical is helpful to us. But as you have noticed, our bodies do feel younger—a wonderful perk, I'd say—and your perceptions become even sharper.

"You will see and hear sights and sounds and even meet people—actually, if you want to be more accurate, *beings*—you never knew existed before. Honey, you're going to have a blast with that part!" Lydia laughed and slapped Rebecca's knee. In her enthusiasm, her voice rose to a higher pitch. "None of your field studies prepared you for this!"

"Oh, dear, I'm getting ahead of myself." Lydia patted Rebecca's knee more softly. "I have to confess, sweetheart, I'm so excited to see you, I'm telling you everything at once! I know you're going to be fascinated by it all, and I just can't stop myself! You're going to learn things that I have no idea about. You'll have opportunities to examine the life you just left, to discuss your mistakes and successes. But don't worry, honey, it's not the throne of judgment like some people expect. You should see how stumped some people are when they arrive and can't find that throne! I hope this doesn't sound mean—I don't intend it to be—but sometimes it makes me giggle. It's all about learning, forgiving, growing, celebrating; it's about discovering how deeply loved we are and how capable we are of loving on a much more profound level than we ever knew. It's about discovering something so large and deep and wonderful that I couldn't possibly explain it to you. It is for you to discover on your own. You won't believe how much fun you're going to have with all this."

Lydia's eyes sparkled as she spoke in animated tones, but now she turned serious and softened her tone. "I can assure you that there is deep peace in all of it too. But I know that you have a particular concern. You want to tell me about that?"

Rebecca felt her mind clear. "Yes. I need to make sure Hannah is going to be okay. I … I didn't know … I didn't know I'd be gone from her so soon." Suddenly, a new thought entered her mind. "Oh! I was going to sew new curtains for her this weekend!" She grasped Lydia's arm. "Hannah and I found this fabric! It had forest elves dancing on a leafy green background. Hannah *loves* forest elves! How will she get her elf curtains now?" Rebecca began to cry.

Lydia spoke softly to her. "You and Reuben left Kate and Mike in charge of taking care of Hannah if anything ever happened to you, right?"

"Yes, but …."

"You didn't think the need would ever really arise, did you?"

Rebecca felt more tears, and could only shake her head and sink into Lydia's shoulder.

"Take a breath, sweetheart," Lydia spoke softly as she placed her hand on Rebecca's heart.

Rebecca took a breath, not a very deep one. She tried again, and this time managed a slower, deeper inhale. As she exhaled slowly, she felt a warm healing glow come from Lydia's hand into her heart. She leaned into Lydia and let the feeling spread.

"Kate will find the fabric, dear. She'll remember your conversation about it. All will be well."

Rebecca felt the warm healing continue to spread through her, and now felt that, even if Kate didn't find the fabric, everything would be all right anyway. Somehow, everything would be okay.

They sat in silence for a few minutes before Rebecca spoke. "I … I want her to feel secure and loved, no matter what. I need to do everything I can. Is that okay? Is that possible?"

"Yes, it is indeed." Lydia nodded. "And *of course* it's okay for you to do this. I got ahead of myself again, when I was talking about all that you would learn. That probably didn't help things just now. Let me get to the important point here: before you can concentrate on new ideas, you need to experience Reassurance. Even though you've been healed of your major fears—and the rest will disappear soon, too—you need reassurance so that you can replace those missing fears with calm and joyful courage. This is what will make it easier to learn new things. I know that when you set out to find your reassurance—in your case, about Hannah—you will accomplish this easily." She looked thoughtfully into Rebecca's eyes. "And, in no time at all, you will be achieving *other* things you never dreamed were possible."

*　　　　　*　　　　　*

Reuben heard his mom's voice: "Alright, Reuben! You can

do it!" The bases were loaded. This was his big chance. Reuben would save the day.

"Whack!" A perfect hit. He ran, surprised at his speed, his buoyancy. His team, other twelve-year-old boys, ran with him. Suddenly, they were in the air, soaring, dipping, floating in a sky filled with colors he'd never seen before, beyond the colors of the rainbow he thought he knew. These he could not describe, and felt no need to. He paused midair, and found himself softly floating downward until he landed lightly on his feet and took stock of his surroundings. No baseball diamond in sight, the team forgotten, he stood on grass that sprawled for acres. Sycamores showed off new-green leaves, squirrels darted around the trunks, and only a few puffs of white drifted in the blue sky.

"More fun than making a home run?" The amusement in his mother's voice was unmistakable.

"Mom?" Reuben looked around.

"Over here." His mom—in her favorite floral-print pedal pushers, faded navy sweatshirt, beat-up tennis shoes, and an aqua bandana to keep her hair out of her eyes—wiped red and yellow paint from her hands and two slim paintbrushes with a splotchy towel. She slipped the paintbrushes into one back pocket, towel into the other, as she walked toward him. Reuben found himself enveloped in her hug. He hugged her back in a surge of joy and a sense of home that he hadn't felt in ages. She smelled like lemon blossoms, the way he always remembered her. He sank into her hug as she held onto him, rocking him for a moment.

Finally, she loosened her hug, and gestured with one arm

in introduction. "Do you remember Thaddeus?" she asked.

Reuben saw a man who looked familiar. Tall, slim, and bearded, he wore jeans and a flannel shirt with the sleeves rolled up. Instinctively, Reuben put his hand to his own face.

"I have a beard!" he exclaimed. "I … what …." he stopped, confused.

Reuben's mother and Thaddeus chuckled kindly.

"I thought I was, I don't know. I feel like I'm twelve! How can I have a beard? What's going on?" He tried to get his bearings. He looked back at his mother. "Mom!" His mother had died five years ago. Now he was beginning to remember. The car. Rebecca. Goosebumps crept up his arms, up his neck, tingling his scalp. Strangely, though, he didn't feel afraid. Only confused. "I died …." he said, staring at his hands.

"That's not what we call it here. For obvious reasons." Reuben's mom smiled with compassion. "But yes, that's what we used to call it." She rested her hand on his shoulder for a moment to let this sink in before she spoke again. "I'm here to ease your entry, honey. But Thaddeus is going to be your guide and get you oriented. He's been at this much longer than I have."

Reuben peered more closely at Thaddeus. "Wait. *Grandpa?*" He hadn't seen his grandfather since college, but now he looked much younger than when Reuben had known him. They'd taken camping trips together from the time Reuben was four years old. Grandpa had been a veterinarian at the San Francisco Zoo. He had let Reuben come with him sometimes during the summer to help him with his rounds, which got young Reuben interested in biology. They wrote letters and talked on the phone while Reuben was in college. Grandpa had died three weeks before Reuben graduated, and Reuben had felt miserable through the entire ceremony. He had wanted so badly for Grandpa to be there.

His grandfather seemed to know what Reuben was thinking. "I've been very proud of you, Reuben. You made a good choice to teach. It suited you."

Reuben smiled back at his grandpa. Thaddeus. Reuben turned to his mom. "Mom, why are you calling your own father by his first name?"

Thaddeus chuckled and put his hand on his forehead. "There's a lot to explain, and we're both bumbling it pretty badly. We plead mercy! It's just that we're happy as clams at high water to see you, so we've forgotten that some incremental information would be more helpful. I apologize, since I'm the one who's been here longer and should know better. At any rate, the definitions we worked within before … over there … don't have as much meaning here. Our roles change, and even though it seems confusing at first, we find it actually simpler to just use first names, no matter what the relationship was before."

"But even though you can call me Rose now if you want, some things haven't changed," his mom asserted with a smile and a tug at Reuben's elbow. "Before you start your tour, let's get something to eat."

Reuben found himself at a picnic table with Mom—Rose—and Thaddeus. (It felt easier to adjust to calling his grandfather by his first name. Changing how he addressed his mom might take some time.) Piled high on a plate in the middle of the table were several chili dogs, Reuben's favorite, which he had sworn off years ago because of those horrifying ingredients. But, oh, he had missed them! Rose laughed at Reuben, clearly enjoying the hungry look on his face. "You can eat all you want here, sweetheart!" she chuckled. "Nutrition, or lack thereof, is irrelevant here." To set the tone, Thaddeus swung one leg over the picnic bench and grabbed a chili dog before he was completely seated. Reuben sat and dug in. Savory sauce stewed with chunks of beef and pinto beans smothered a hot dog that tasted like real meat—a combination of pork and beef, slightly smoky, and a delicious tang he couldn't quite identify. It warmed him before he had even swallowed the first bite. He closed his eyes to focus on the flavors, and emitted several appreciative grunts. When he opened his eyes again, he found a cold mug of beer waiting for him. He took a big gulp and sighed in utter satisfaction at such decadence. The contrast among the flavors and temperatures thrilled him. He smiled and shook his head between bites and swigs, grinning at his mom. When he had eaten and drunk all he wanted, he discovered French vanilla ice cream waiting for him with thick hot fudge, whipped cream, and a big spoon. He dug in, finding he had plenty of room for his favorite dessert.

He looked across the table at his mom, who, he just noticed, was eating linguini with scallops and prawns in a white wine garlic sauce, which had always been one of her favorites, along with a glass of Pinot Grigio.

"Don't worry," she said, after swallowing, her eyes twinkling. "No shellfish were harmed in the making of this experience. No animals died for your meal either. It's just a sensation, for fun."

"Mom ...." he began. Suddenly, though the joy remained, he felt a profound shift in his mood. The meaning of sitting with his mom sunk in. How had he passed by this so quickly a little while ago? Shocked at his obliviousness, he pleaded, "Mom ...."

Now his mom sat next to him, though he hadn't seen her get up and move. She rested her hand on his cheek. "Oh, honey, it's a little boggling, isn't it?"

Reuben felt his throat tighten, but he shook off the feeling. "Well, you *did* seem to be everywhere at once when I was a kid, especially when I thought I was about to get away with something. But this actual disappearing and reappearing stuff is kind of over the top, Mom."

Rose laughed and tousled his hair. Then, with a more serious tone, she cupped her hand under his chin. "You don't need to feel bad about not taking it all in at once. You have to get used to everything, so you are purposely given the ability to perceive only a little at a time. Otherwise, it would be too much."

This made sense to Reuben now. "I remember something before I found myself on the baseball field. It was so peaceful and healing. It felt ... well ... profound. And yet ... personal. And I remember laughing." Reuben tilted his head with a perplexed smile.

Rose nodded, smiling back at him.

"What was that?" he asked.

"What do you think it was?"

"Well, I ...." Reuben hesitated, trying to put words to it. "I felt pain leaving me; I felt this surprising joy. It was, well, this might sound weird coming from me, but it felt like something … so *deep*. I don't even know what that means." He hesitated. "But it was … it was *good*." Reuben shrugged helplessly at not being able to find a description that really said what he wanted to.

"It was, indeed. That's a perfectly good word, honey."

"There's something else though. This might sound trivial after what I just said."

"Go ahead, sweetheart."

"Well, *first*, I think I woke up in my hammock, like the one in my backyard. I always felt so relaxed there. Then the even deeper feelings came of being healed. Does that make sense?"

"Absolutely! That's how it happens. Very personal, profound healing, then laughing." Rose got up and did a few dance steps around the table and came back to Reuben. She gave him a long hug and kissed him on the forehead. "I'll see you later, sweetie. You and Thaddeus have a nice talk now."

"Wait! Mom! Rebecca …." A wave of new realization came to him with an odd blend of tragedy and hope. "Is she here too?"

"Yes, she is. But you need to get acclimated first with Thaddeus for a while; then you'll see her, I promise." Rose waited for a moment, as this new information sunk in.

Becca here. The car crash. How could he not have thought of that first off? *And Hannah! What about Hannah?* He searched his mom's face. "Things really do get foggy, don't they?"

"Only for a while, sweetheart. You'll see." Rose kissed his forehead again. "Don't worry" she assured him. "All is well. There is plenty of time for everything we want to do. I'll see you later." She turned and grabbed an easel and canvas that Reuben hadn't noticed before; she waved happily, and then danced her own version of a walking samba into a grove of trees.

Reuben watched her go. "When did Mom start painting?" he asked Thaddeus.

"Not 'til she got here," Thaddeus replied. "She'd always meant to. Did you know that?"

Reuben hadn't known. What else had escaped his notice?

Thaddeus continued. "There is a lot of that going on here. Life over there gets so frenetic, you can't fit it all in. But you can catch up on all of it here, if it still means something to you."

"Huh. I never knew she wanted to paint."

"Well, don't feel bad. Very often, we get so busy that we push those dreams aside, and forget them ourselves. So most of the time we never say them out loud. Then, when we get here and the fog clears from our minds, we think, 'Oh yeah! *Now* I remember!' And off we go."

"Yes, I can see that," Reuben mused.

"For instance, you've always wanted to scuba dive, am I right?"

"Oh yeah! I forgot!" Reuben and Thaddeus laughed.

"You see? That's exactly how it goes." Thaddeus nodded, remembering his own discoveries.

Reuben sat quietly, reflecting. Finally, he said, "Now that I think about it, yes, I can imagine my mom wanting to paint. But as for that samba I just saw, well, that'll take a little more time."

Thaddeus guffawed and wiped his beard with a napkin. He swung his long legs over the picnic bench to stand. "Let's sit over here."

Reuben followed Thaddeus to a log and looked around. They stood at one of their favorite campsites in a redwood forest next to a large stream. He let the cool earthiness wash over him and he felt himself relax more fully.

Thaddeus watched Reuben's eyes as the relaxation sank in. "Good," he nodded. Then he gestured, "Here, sit." They sat on the log, and Thaddeus said, "Ah, check out that stream! Remember all the cool critters we used to find in there?"

Reuben smiled and nodded, knowing he didn't need to say anything. He kept gazing at the water, bubbling over rocks, swooshing through the sticks and leaves caught between larger stones. He thought about his mom painting and the opportunity people had here to do things they never had time to do before. He thought of Rebecca. "You know," he said, "Rebecca always wanted to go to Alaska and see the aurora borealis. I was going to surprise her with a trip there this summer."

"Ah, yes. A popular pastime here. Some people take lawn chairs and watch it while they eat popcorn. A friend of mine discovered that you can dive right into it, and even dance on all the colors. Rebecca will have that opportunity if she wants it. You both will."

Reuben pictured the delight he would see in Rebecca's face when she discovered the aurora borealis for the first time, and found himself filled with a surge of longing to see her.

"You'll see her soon," Thaddeus confirmed, as if he knew his grandson's thoughts. "It might not seem like it yet, but later you'll see that it is helpful for you to slow down and discover things on your own before you see each other."

Reuben nodded, trying to get used to this idea.

"It will help you now to know three important things." Thaddeus held up his first finger. "One: there is plenty of time."

He touched his second finger. "Two: all is well." Touching the third finger, he concluded, "And three: whatever we do here, whatever we talk about, however long it takes, it is the same as a *millisecond* on the earthly plane."

Reuben scrutinized Thaddeus's face. "Really?"

"Really. Now, sorry if this sounds condescending, but I want you to repeat those three things back to me. They're important."

Reuben repeated them, feeling like a little boy again, but he trusted his grandfather completely, and this made him feel more secure. Then, his head full of so much new information, Reuben bent forward to untie his shoes.

"I've just got to feel that water," he said.

"Excellent idea, boy," said Thaddeus, who began to untie his own shoes.

When Reuben had one shoe off, he started to set it aside. But suddenly, his ears rang with a strange realization. With the shoe still mid-air, he looked sideways at Thaddeus. He repeated softly, "There's plenty of time and all is well." He tried to concentrate. "Where have I heard that before?"

Thaddeus gave him a sly grin.

"Wait. I think Mom said that before she left."

Thaddeus nodded.

"But ...." Reuben tried to concentrate. "But I have this feeling. Have *you* said that to me before?"

"Yes, I have." He held eye contact with Reuben and his grin grew more mischievous. "Yes, I have," he said more slowly, as if waiting for Reuben to catch up.

"But, I haven't seen you in years! I mean, until today."

"True."

"Okay. Now this is getting weird." Reuben shook his head.

"Don't worry about what's weird, Reuben. Just say what's on your mind. Trust yourself."

"Well … I had a dream a few years ago. Before Hannah was born. It was when I was stressed about the pregnancy and having to give up my plans to travel."

Thaddeus nodded. "That was me. You're not crazy."

"You told me there was plenty of time and all was well. I remember now. It felt so *real*."

"That's because it was."

Reuben shook his head again. He reached for his other shoe and pulled it off. "Okay, now I really need to concentrate on something normal." He headed for the stream. Thaddeus followed. They sat on a large flat rock and dangled their bare feet in the cool water.

Ruben sighed with relief to have the simplicity of this moment. Minnows shimmied around their feet and, on the calmer surface near the banks, water striders made tiny foot dents. Listening to the water tumble over rocks upstream and smelling the damp earth and redwood essence helped him to see the jumble of Thaddeus's words in a simpler way. After only a few minutes, he didn't feel overwhelmed anymore. "So, people can really come to you in a dream?"

Thaddeus nodded.

"You can help people, long distance."

Thaddeus smiled at him. "Well, not as long distance as you might imagine."

"Hm. Well, I'm not going to try to think too hard about

that right now. I feel like it will come more clear when I need it to."

"That's the spirit!"

"But, thanks for what you did. It helped."

"You're welcome."

The two men watched the stream in silence for a while. Reuben marveled that, though he remained a bit confused, he also felt a new feeling he'd rarely had before—a relaxed awareness that he would learn what he needed to at the right time. But this didn't put a damper on his curiosity.

"So, Grandpa … Thaddeus." Reuben gave Thaddeus the same squint-eyed slight-smile he always had when he felt he was onto something. "Tell me more about milliseconds on the earthly plane."

"Ahhh." Thaddeus nodded appreciatively. He had been playing with a thin redwood branch in the stream, watching the water rush around it. He tossed it aside and brushed off his hands. "Okay. Here's a relevant example: how long do you think you've been here?"

"Wow … I don't know. Let's see. I had that healing experience in the hammock; hard to say how long that was. Seemed like a long time. I played baseball. I had lunch with you and Mom. A day? Two days?"

Thaddeus inclined his head toward him and said, "You know your old Corvette that flipped upside down against a tree?"

"Yeah?"

"The wheels are still spinning."

*   *   *

Rebecca and Lydia sank into the couch in Lydia's garden. They rested their heads on the back cushions and closed their eyes to the sun. Rebecca thought she heard music. At first, it was faint, but gradually the volume grew. She knew that song, but couldn't quite place it. Full orchestra, strings, slow, full, moving. Ah! Barber's "Adagio." Beautiful!

She kept her eyes closed and murmured, "Where is that music coming from, Lydia?"

"Oh," Lydia laughed. "It's Helen. She's a good friend of mine. I'll introduce you to her one of these days. Right now, I can guarantee you she's enjoying a big bowl of fresh strawberries, too. She loves to eat strawberries—with whipped cream—while she listens to Barber's 'Adagio.' She says they are 'glorious' together." Lydia laughed again kindly, as Rebecca lifted her head to give her an amused look. "And," she instructed with mock seriousness, "mint chip ice cream goes best with Ray Charles."

Rebecca laughed and shook her head. What would she hear next?

"We won't visit her just yet. She likes to have the full experience uninterrupted."

Lydia and Rebecca rested their heads against the back of the couch once more, and reveled in the music.

*   *   *

Picturing the wheels of his car still spinning—someplace light years from here, as far as he could figure—Reuben pulled off his clothes and plunged into the water. It was pleasantly cool. A few feet from the edge, the streambed dropped to several feet deep, enough to immerse himself completely. He submerged his head and concentrated on the comforting pressure of the just-right water that surrounded him. He swam upstream, then lay suspended underwater for a while before righting himself and opening his eyes.

"Whew!" he blew, and pushed back his hair. "I needed that." He climbed out. He put his clothes back on and said with conviction, "I have to find Rebecca. And I need to know if Hannah is okay."

"Yes." Thaddeus stood. "Let's get you started." He pointed his long arm toward a mountain trail nearby. "We need to follow this trail, first. You up for that?"

Reuben felt ready to climb Everest. "Let's go!" He strode forward, and even though his legs were much shorter than Thaddeus's, he had no trouble keeping up. They climbed a slope, and were soon surrounded by evergreens, oaks, and large rocks. The sun was warm enough to make the pines emit their sweet fragrance. Reuben took it in and reflected. He had just been killed, and yet he knew, for reasons he couldn't fathom, that everything would be all right. This made no sense to him. And here he was, walking next to his grandfather, who looked younger than he had ever known him. He needed to see Rebecca. He needed to know if Hannah would be alright. But even with this sense of urgency, he wasn't upset.

Downy woodpeckers, dark-eyed juncos, nuthatches, and

black-capped chickadees hopped through the underbrush and swooped from tree to tree, calling to one another; some, it seemed to Reuben, singing just for fun. Lizards darted among the rocks. "What a great trail," he said.

"Yes, this is right up your alley, isn't it? You see, when anyone first arrives here, their experience is individualized for their particular soul's needs. No matter what part of the earth you came from, what culture, or what religion, the environment that you perceive is one that feels familiar, welcoming, and safe for you—whatever makes your heart feel at ease. For you, it was your backyard hammock. And this trail, and other favorite experiences." Thaddeus gave Reuben his familiar one-eyebrow-raised smile. "For instance, you certainly enjoyed your lunch."

Reuben grinned. "Yes, I did."

"Later, as you feel more at home, your environment expands; you get to explore other people's perceptions of where we are, what makes them happy. I have to say, I always get a real kick out of doing that. It's fascinating, and the more I explore, the more nuances I catch. And I've made some good friends in the process."

Reuben thought for a moment, and asked, "So, Grandpa, where did you find yourself when you got here?"

"I found myself in a tree fort in the wintertime, back in Oregon. I stuck my head out, and a snowball whizzed past my ear. My brother had thrown it. But," he grinned slyly, "That's a story for another day."

Reuben smiled, content that, eventually, he would hear the story.

"But, of course, the greatest thing that takes place is the

first one—when fear is removed. This enabled you to rest as deeply as you did in your hammock. Then you are healed of whatever it is that ended your life on earth. In the same way, any mental and emotional illnesses, large and small, are healed. Not much was necessary for you, except for the little tweaks we all need, but this is when it happens. Pain is healed in layers over time, since it helps our understanding if we can observe what is happening in stages. But *all* pain will eventually be healed completely."

Two squirrels ran up a pine tree as Thaddeus continued. "After they've been healed of their fear and then greeted, people typically begin to examine the life that they just left. We call this our Exploration in Empathy. One event at a time, you relive everything you ever said or did; but this time, it is from the point of view of the people you said or did it to. This new empathy expands beyond what you were ever able to experience before. Now, you understand the effect you had on others. You understand how they felt. And how they are currently feeling."

Reuben stopped and frowned. Although he'd always tried to be easy to get along with, he could think of plenty of times he'd been unpleasant to people. These were not moments he wanted to revisit.

"Aha!" Thaddeus stopped too. He smiled and pointed at Reuben. "I see that you are automatically thinking of all the negative things you did, whether they were downright mean or more trivial oversights. What we are all surprised to discover is that of all the people we might need to forgive from our past, it is actually hardest to forgive ourselves. But this is a time to remember *everything*. This means that you remember all the good that you did, as well. Part of your healing is to remember the good things, to understand how hard human beings are on themselves. There is so much good we did that we actually block it from our memories—if you can believe that. This is the place where you will find such hidden treasure."

Reuben considered this.

"Trust me," Thaddeus assured Reuben. "You won't really be spending eternity examining the life you just left. It will take no time at all, in the big picture. So relax and savor the experience. It makes all other experiences richer. You'll be amazed at the great moments you've forgotten and the kind things you did absentmindedly. It makes some people laugh out loud in surprise. It's a tremendous relief when misunderstandings are cleared up, because very often what we thought was a bad thing was not, or what we thought was a good thing was not. We see things as they really were for others as well as for ourselves."

Something nagged at Reuben, but before he could put his finger on it, Thaddeus continued.

"But in cases like yours and Rebecca's, sometimes the exploration in empathy is delayed in favor of finding Reassurance. Even though you have been healed of fear, your sense of responsibility to the life you just left stays foremost in your mind, and it's harder to concentrate on your exploration until you find the reassurance for yourself that all is well. This is almost always true for the parents of small children."

Yes, Reuben thought. *That's what I've been feeling.*

"This is something that is always readily granted to anyone who asks for it. Clearly, this is what you want to do, and I imagine that Rebecca will want to, as well."

Reuben knew this was true. "Yes. I'm sure she will."

Thaddeus patted Reuben's shoulder and continued to walk. "You can rest easy, in that, my boy. Now as you can imagine, there is much more to learn, but let's change gears to something more lighthearted. You need a chance to set all this aside and play. Remember, there is plenty of time. The more you take your time and savor each moment, the more you will see that all is well and all is unfolding with perfect timing. And as a teacher, you know that while you're learning a load of new material, it's crucial to take a break and have some fun. It's good for the soul, too." He stopped at a beautiful wooden lodge with a stone chimney and—knowing what would happen next—grinned at Reuben as the double doors opened for them.

"He's here! He's here!" Reuben heard one voice shout out, then another and another. Before he could identify the voices or prepare for the thumpity-rumbling coming toward him, heavy, furry masses struck him in the chest and knocked him on his back. He hit the ground hard. It didn't hurt, but the impact knocked the wind out of him for a moment. He gasped and got it back, just in time before slathery tongues and warm humid doggy breath ambushed his lips, his cheeks, his eyelids. He couldn't tell how many furry bodies pounced over his chest and stomach. Miraculously, he could still breathe with the weight of them all. Something tugged at his pant leg. "Come on, come *on*! Let's *go*!" a voice at his feet shouted happily.

Reuben finally managed to sit up. He realized that, along with the barking-snuffling noises, he could hear Thaddeus laughing. But all he could see were the faces of three dogs—dogs he'd had when he was growing up.

"Lucy!" His golden retriever, who had died when Reuben was fourteen, answered Reuben by putting both front paws on Reuben's shoulders. Somehow, he managed to stay upright. He looked into Lucy's face and rubbed her ears, her face, her neck. She gave him her best laughing dog face. Then she said, "Reuben! Reuben! I've missed you! Reuben! I thought you'd never get here! Reuben! Wait 'til I show you everything I've found!" She gave him another lick of joy.

Reuben laughed, then just stared openmouthed at Lucy. A muddled thought occurred to him that he was having more trouble finding words than his own dog. Then it hit him. His dog was speaking in a language he understood. Her voice sounded sort of like a human woman's, only a bit wilder, less refined. He caught a glimpse of Thaddeus through the bouncing dogs. He was just a few feet away, leaning against the wall, arms crossed casually, enjoying the scene. When Reuben made eye contact, Thaddeus shrugged and grinned. "Welcome to Heaven," he said.

Bullwinkle, a Great Dane-Lab mix, barked loudly and galloped awkward circles around Reuben and the others, saying, "Oh, boy! Oh, boy! Oh, boy!" in a bass voice, between large barks before diving in (giving Lucy's head a friendly shove) for another face slurp. Reuben rubbed Bullwinkle's head with one hand, as he put his other arm around Lucy, who threw herself against Reuben's side and smiled up at him.

"Rocky!" Reuben called out when he could see through the others to find the source of tugging at his pant leg, though he knew who it was before he looked. This was how Rocky—a corgi-basset mix—always told him it was time to go out and play. He'd been Reuben's dog from the time he was a baby until he was ten. Rocky and Lucy had been great friends. Bullwinkle came into Reuben's life after Rocky and Lucy had died, and even stayed with him in his apartment in college, until they got a new landlord and Bullwinkle had to go back home to Reuben's parents.

Rocky let go of the spitty jeans and panted a bright-eyed smile at Reuben. He ducked his head and jumped to the side.

"Are you surprised? We hid in here to surprise you! Were you surprised?" he asked in a voice close to a tenor, with just a touch of a gravelly texture to it.

Reuben reached down to pet Rocky all over. "Bowled over! I've missed you all, too!" he laughed, his voice breaking. Tears of joy and relief spilled down his face.

"We're crazy about Bullwinkle!" Lucy enthused. "You made a great choice when you picked him after we were gone."

Rocky agreed, "We kept an eye on you, after we left, you know. We saw that you were sad, and we hoped you'd get another dog soon. We liked Bullwinkle right away, and when he got here, we headed up his welcoming committee!" Rocky puffed out his chest. "You know, humans do better if they are greeted by only one or two people at a time, but dogs—well, you know, we're pack animals, after all—we like to be greeted by a *group*."

"Rocky and Lucy were great!" Bullwinkle chimed in with

a sincere face, his jowls flapping in punctuation that added muffleyness to his articulation. "I didn't know them before, though I think I had some dreams about them, so they seemed a bit familiar when I arrived. We became close friends right away, and we loved comparing stories about you." The three dogs looked at each other in the same way that people do when they share special memories.

Reuben tilted his head for a moment, wondering about this, then laughed. "I'm so happy to see you characters again!"

"Let's go outside now!" Rocky wiggled his rear end and pranced in place. "You want to, Reuben? Let's go run around!"

Reuben laughed. "Of course!" He stood up and headed for the double doors that opened for them.

As the dogs romped in circles around Reuben's legs and he somehow never tripped, Lucy panted happily and said, "You know the best thing about this place? I mean, besides *you* being here now?"

"What's that?" Reuben smiled at her.

"You can roll in something reeeally stinky, and nobody yells at you."

*　　　*　　　*

Lydia led Rebecca along the damp forest path, springy with brown redwood needles. Rebecca's heart felt full and happy. "That was astonishing!" she exclaimed to Lydia. "I had no idea a guinea pig could be that brilliant."

Lydia laughed. "She was so glad to see you, at first she was speechless, which is very rare for Gertrude, I have to say."

"So, you two have talked before?"

"My dear, your guinea pig and I have had many a philosophical discussion over the years. She has provided me with some wonderful insights that I don't think would ever have occurred to me, no matter how long I lived here. She has an extraordinary point of view."

"Well, I can see that. Now that I'm over the shock, at least, *mostly* anyway." Rebecca paused and shook her head. "Sweet little Gertrude. To think I used to talk such nonsense to her when I was a child." She laughed.

"Don't worry, she understood, even then. Guinea pigs have a strong sense of perspective."

"By the way, Lydia, how is it that Gertrude and I can communicate so clearly now?"

"Isn't that marvelous? It's because the atmosphere here is different, and allows for brain functions—actually, to be more precise, *mind* functions—that weren't possible on earth. You'll find this with everyone here. Even though we all lived in different parts of the world, and even if we spoke different languages there —and in addition to the human languages you're already aware of, dogs have always spoken Doglish, cats Felinian, and guinea pigs Caviidaen— whatever anyone says here automatically translates inside our minds into a language that we understand."

"Ah! I love that!" Rebecca's eyes were bright. "Well, Gertrude says that the next time we get together she'll show me her favorite vegetable patch, and we can talk about what she's been doing since she arrived here. I can't wait to see more from her point of view."

Lydia led them deeper into the forest. The tall redwoods grew closer together now, enveloping them in comfortably cool air. Rebecca stopped to take in the height and aroma of the trees, then she turned to Lydia. "Lydia," she said. "I loved seeing Gertrude, of course. It's not that I didn't enjoy that. But I need to see *Reuben*. When can I see him?"

Lydia put her arm on Rebecca's shoulder as they resumed their walk.

"I know we talked about this already, Lydia. I just … I just need to see him, you know?"

"I understand. Don't ever feel bad for wanting to see someone you love. And now is a good time. You're ready. And as a matter of fact, that's where we're headed right now. So let me tell you what's next: we're going to one of our gathering places, which is used for many purposes. One of the things we do there is ask questions that are not so much about ourselves, but about the life that we left behind. It's not what we'll be doing this time, but it's a place I think you'll enjoy visiting later, so I thought I'd mention it to you now. People ask questions that can be profound or whimsical. Any question is fair game—which sounds like just your style." Lydia beamed at Rebecca. "After you get through your exploration in empathy, answers tend to come more naturally, but for a long time before we grow more adept, we enjoy the questions and discussions."

"What kinds of questions do people ask?" Rebecca brushed her hand across a low soft redwood bough as she walked, then touched the fragrance to her nose.

"When people first arrive, many questions pertain to why they died when they did. Some people even ask about political parties or religious denominations, though you'd be surprised how quickly trivia like that becomes a bore. But we encourage even those questions because that gets them out of the questioner's system more quickly, and helps them to focus on the more interesting and important questions.

"The purpose of *this* gathering is to provide you with support as you seek reassurance. This is a good time to meet others, because it's nourishing to feel encouragement from many, not just from me. We'll explain what you need to know, and give you a blessing to get started."

They came to a clearing. There, several yards away, stood a yurt, covered in woven wool rugs. Curls of smoke rose out of an opening in the center of the roof. The scene felt wonderfully inviting to Rebecca. Lydia walked over to the yurt, lifted the door flap—a soft heavy fabric with an intricate weave—and entered. Rebecca followed close behind, letting the flap drop softly behind them.

Rebecca found herself standing on thick carpeting in a large round room. Tapestries of all styles covered the walls. In the center of the room, a round stone pit contained a small fire. Smoke drew easily up and out through a large opening in the roof, leaving only a soft woodsy fragrance. Around the fire sat about thirty people of all ages and races, who smiled and nodded at Rebecca. She also noticed some shiny undulating ovals of rainbowish light, about the same size as a person, here and there in the crowd. No, oval wasn't it, Rebecca thought.

Ovals were too regular. These were more like clouds, though they were more transparent than that. They were more like mist, vaguely contained. Their glow seemed to increase momentarily when she looked at them. Rebecca wondered if they were the more advanced people that Lydia had mentioned to her, who no longer had a physical body. Somehow she felt that the increased glowing she saw could be them smiling at her. Fascinated, she smiled back at them and kept wondering. *Hmm, what am I supposed to call them? The "colorful-mist people"? That sounds too weird. Maybe just "advanced beings," since I'm pretty sure that's what they are. I'll ask Lydia.*

Just then, the door flap opened again. Rebecca turned, and felt a rush of joy. There stood Reuben. With a gasp, he leapt forward and caught Rebecca in his arms. As he swung her around, she hung on to him, laughing. All around them, the others chuckled affectionately.

Reuben and Rebecca slowed and released each other for a moment, and held each other's gaze. They hugged again, more tightly, before looking at each other again, beaming. They searched each other's eyes, and each somehow knew what the other had already learned. They embraced again for a long time, letting it all soak in. Finally, they turned and, holding hands, looked at the group.

Their attention turned to a bronze-skinned woman sitting in the circle. Her dark wavy hair had white streaks in it and cascaded freely to her waist. She smiled, crinkling her slightly almond eyes. "Welcome, Rebecca and Reuben. I'm Mahina."

They smiled and nodded at her. Mahina's soft alto voice reminded Rebecca of a low-pitched pan flute. She felt a surge of affection for Mahina, though she hardly knew why. She had never met her before, of course. On the other hand, she felt that somehow they knew each other well. She turned to Reuben to say this to him, but Mahina spoke again. "I know that you are eager to catch up with each other. You'll have plenty of time to do that shortly. As I'm sure Lydia and Thaddeus have told you, this is often a place for questions and discussion. But we also use it as a place in which to gather oneself before the first time we travel."

Her open arms warmly gestured Rebecca and Reuben toward the circle, and they sat on the luxurious carpeting, with Thaddeus and Lydia on either side of them.

"I imagine it's been frustrating for you to wait this long, when you've both wanted to visit Hannah since you got here. But there is good reason for this delay. It helps to acclimate first to this new 'climate,' for lack of a better term. If you rushed to visit Earth before that, its atmosphere would be too confusing to you. Now you have a much better handle on things, even if you might not realize it.

"Please know that we are here for you today. We'd like to encourage you to relax and regroup. Take in all that you have learned so far. You are welcome to ask questions any time. But we encourage you to breathe in the silence for a while before you begin. Be assured that you are not keeping us from anything. We are exactly where we want to be."

Rebecca closed her eyes. She did, indeed, need to catch up with herself. She inhaled slowly, took in the warmth of the fire, and exhaled easily. The love in the room felt profoundly nourishing. She let all that she had seen and learned soak in.

She found it remarkably easy to let go of her need to understand anything. She knew that answers would come if she needed them. And yet she knew with wonderment and gratitude that she already understood more than she had expected to. Without effort, the thought came to her: *there is plenty of time, and all is well.* And for the first time, she truly believed it. She breathed in again, allowing for mysteries, strength, energy, and peace. As she exhaled and held Reuben's hand, she knew that he was experiencing these same feelings. Feeling him next to her, she felt a new surge of deep joy.

She opened her eyes and turned to Reuben. He had just opened his, as well. They looked more deeply into each other's eyes, and this seemed to integrate their new extraordinary circumstances with the old familiarity of each other. Then they turned to Mahina.

"We're ready," Reuben said.

"Eli?" Mahina held her arm out to a wiry little man. Unlike most everyone they'd met here so far, he looked old and shriveled, but he looked as happy as those who chose to wear their youth. He wore a tan sleeveless tunic made of what looked like suede, with a thin woven cord tied at the waist, and sandals. His eyes shone in a bright lavender tone, and his smile was broad and genuine. Wispy white hair exploded from his head in odd amounts and angles.

"Hello, Rebecca and Reuben. I'm Eli," he said, as he came over to sit across from them.

"Hi, Eli." Rebecca held out her hand, which he shook happily. As his smile broadened, Rebecca felt that she saw tiny flashes of multicolored light emanating from his eyes, but she couldn't say for certain, and the sensation disappeared quickly. But she watched as Reuben shook Eli's hand, and saw him squint with interest at Eli's eyes, too.

Eli settled in and looked back and forth between Rebecca and Reuben. "Though your arrival here might seem to you as if it were long ago, it has still only been a millisecond on the earthly plane. No one there knows yet that you've made this leap. That is a gift for you, so you can get your bearings before you visit."

Rebecca felt herself relax more deeply. Yes, now that Lydia, Mahina, and Eli had all explained this concept to her, she felt the sense of it in a more solid way.

Eli continued. "You want to visit your daughter, am I correct?"

"Yes," Reuben replied.

"We want to see Hannah and make sure she will always know that we love her, no matter what has happened." Rebecca said.

"And to make sure she's well cared for, and that she has everything she needs to grow up happy and fulfilled," Reuben continued.

Eli said gently, "You do know that bumps in the road happen over there, and it is part of our learning."

"Yes," Reuben said. "I know that I already feel more at peace here than I could have imagined, but I sure don't feel like I have the hang of it altogether. I still worry about my daughter. I can't stop wanting to see her and be with her."

Eli nodded sympathetically.

"I hope that's not wrong to want that," Reuben added.

"A desire is never wrong when it is motivated by love," Eli assured him. "It is perfectly natural for a loving parent to feel unsettled, even here. You need not feel embarrassed about any emotions that pull you."

Reuben took Rebecca's hand. "Thank you," he said to Eli.

Eli bowed slightly in acknowledgement. "Okay. Before we start, it is my responsibility to tell you that this is your home now, and I can promise you that you will find joy and peace here. Knowing this will make the next important aspect easier to get used to—that yes, absolutely, you can visit the earthly plane any time. But you cannot stay there indefinitely. They are only visits. This is your home now. Do you understand?"

Reuben and Rebecca nodded, both finding that this did not alarm them as they might have expected.

"Good." Eli folded his hands and leaned forward. "I believe that you both will adapt to this new experience rapidly, but I will tell you some important practical things that you need to know ahead of time."

Rebecca and Reuben again nodded, and he continued. "First of all, when you visit, you will find that most people cannot see you. But very often, babies and animals *can* see you, or hear you, or both—in the form in which they remember you. With a child Hannah's age, we've seen some who can see us and some who cannot. Even though you are no longer a physical body, you will be able to touch her because you are feeling her on an energetic level. And—again because Hannah is so young—it is *possible* that she will be able to feel your touch, to what extent, if at all, you will discover over time. Probably the best advice is to watch her face carefully and take it slowly.

As long as your motivation is love, all will go well.

"Now here is the thing you need to keep in mind: even though *technically* it is possible to pick her up, we must ask you not to do this. Of course, this is a very difficult rule for any of us to follow, especially when we visit someone that we love as deeply as you both love Hannah. It helps to know ahead of time that these feelings will occur. And it also makes it easier if you consider it on a practical level: how would it look if you were holding Hannah and someone came into the room? To an adult's vision, Hannah would appear to be floating midair. There is no way for people to reconcile that sort of thing. And so we must be the ones to adapt."

Rebecca nodded, but she could feel her throat tighten. She knew that she already desperately longed to hold Hannah. What would happen when she actually saw her? Could she stick with this rule to not pick her up? She wondered how Reuben was taking this, but he was staring downward, his brow furrowed. She looked to Lydia, who was watching her with concern.

"I know it feels impossible, dear. But you will find the strength. It will be easier than you think in this moment. It might help to keep in mind that you can visit as often as you want, and we recommend that you make your first visit short, just to get used to it. It helps to come back and ponder it for a while, to regroup, if you will."

"Yes," Eli added, smiling. "Remember, there is plenty of time, and all is well." He stood, and Rebecca and Reuben followed his lead as he lifted the yurt flap and walked outside.

Mahina and the others followed and gathered around them. "We offer our love and support as you embark on your visit," she said. "Go with joy." All the people held their palms up to them in blessing. The opalescent light of the advanced beings became brighter. Rebecca and Reuben felt their anxieties vanish. Fresh peace and energy washed over them. Revitalized, they hugged each other.

"It's going to be okay," Reuben said with calm conviction, holding her in his arms.

"Yes," Rebecca said with a new assuredness. She hugged him a bit longer, soaking in the renewed sense of calm. Finally, they both smiled and turned to Eli.

Eli watched them for a moment and then nodded, apparently satisfied. He placed a hand on each of their heads. "You now have the ability to relocate as you see fit," he declared.

A new sensation coursed through them. Warm energy turned to a lovely soft pulsating that surrounded their bodies. They looked at each other, bug-eyed.

"Wow," Reuben said in a stage whisper.

"Boggling," Rebecca laughed.

Then they absorbed what this meant and their excitement soared. "Hannah!" they shouted.

The soft pulsating became more apparent to them. They could hear Thaddeus say, (though he didn't sound as close by as he had been) "You're on your way! We'll see you soon." And Lydia, more distant still, said, "Just listen to your hearts." Lydia, Thaddeus, and everyone else faded from their sight.

Rebecca and Reuben could still see each other's faces, but they also saw faint opalescent light shimmering all around them. Before they had a chance to register these perceptions, different objects became clearer. Now, rather than forest floor, they stood on carpeting in Kate and Mike's bedroom, and the next moment, Hannah's sweet sleeping face came into focus.

A rush of euphoria filled Rebecca at the sight of her daughter. She could hear Reuben gulp audibly, that sound he always made when emotion caught him. She rushed over to the little bed that Kate had set up for the evening in the corner of the master bedroom. Rebecca smiled at the memory of Hannah's habit of flopping out of bed and felt a fresh surge of gratitude that Kate—as she always did when she babysat Hannah—had arranged pillows and quilts around her mattress on the floor. Rebecca knelt next to Hannah, partly covered with a quilt. She lay sprawled on her back, her head lolled to one side, mouth slightly open, and arms flopped on either side, every muscle completely relaxed. Rebecca gasped in wonderment at her baby. Hannah was almost two and a half now. Only a few days earlier, they had played hide-and-seek with Ellen. Hannah loved hiding. She had grabbed Ellen's hand, and they scampered into her bedroom. Hannah covered both their faces with part of a quilt, assuming that they were now well hidden, since her own eyes were covered. Rebecca meandered through the house, pretending to search, then finally in mock-surprise, discovered them.

"Momma, you always find me!" Hannah had declared.

Now Rebecca stroked her daughter's cheek. In her sleep, Hannah smiled. Rebecca could feel the impossibly soft skin against her fingers. Automatically, she reached to pick her up, scooping one hand under her baby's head, the other under her hips.

But she caught herself in time.

"Ohh," Rebecca's heart sank. How could she follow this new rule and not pick up her child? She felt suddenly heavy, and collapsed onto the bed next to Hannah. She began to cry.

Reuben's face mirrored Rebecca's grief. He knelt down next to the bed and put his arms around her. "We knew this would be hard," he said.

"I know it has to be this way," she said. "I understand the reasons. It will just take some getting used to, I guess."

She took a deep breath and held it for a moment before letting it out in heavy resignation. "More adjustment," she said softly.

"Yes," Reuben said quietly. He got up from where he had been on his knees next to Rebecca and climbed onto the bed on the other side of Hannah. He began to play with the little curls on her forehead, his face close to hers. Hannah opened her eyes and looked directly into Reuben's. She smiled. She had most of her teeth now, and Reuben never stopped feeling captivated by how tiny and white they were. He smiled tenderly back at her.

Rebecca felt the love and support from the group in the yurt newly fortifying her. Watching Reuben and Hannah now, a flicker of optimism dared to show itself, and she laughed softly.

Hannah turned at the sound and gave Rebecca a smile. With tears of relief and joy, Rebecca snuggled closer to Hannah, her laughter soon muffled in Hannah's sweet neck. Hannah giggled. Rebecca hugged her harder, close to her chest, and kissed the top of her head, again and again.

Reuben took one of Hannah's hands and kissed it while Rebecca stroked Hannah's face. Eventually, they both settled on either side of Hannah, simply inhaling their baby's warm sweetness. Hannah drifted into sleep for a few minutes, then opened her eyes again. She looked back and forth between her parents. Then she focused on something across the room. They turned and saw a shimmering light that soon came into focus as Lydia.

"Ooooh!" Hannah wiggled her fingers at the light around Lydia. Rebecca and Reuben laughed.

"You brilliant child, you," Reuben said to her.

Lydia laughed too. "I had a feeling Hannah would be one who could see." Then her tone became gentle. "Since this is your first visit, it would be a good idea to come back so we can talk it over a bit. You also need some extra fortification for your next visit. Don't worry. You can return again soon." Lydia faded from sight. Hannah blinked, and looked at her parents.

Rebecca snuggled closer to Hannah. Of course, she knew she wanted Hannah always this close. But she was surprised to find that she felt more peace about leaving her for now than she would have expected. She looked at Reuben, trying to figure out how to express this.

"I know," he said quietly. "I feel like it's all okay. It really will be all right. I never would have believed that."

"And we'll be back soon," Rebecca added. "It's that millisecond thing. We don't have to miss anything."

"Right."

"Good night, my dear one," Rebecca whispered to Hannah

the same words she had used each night since Hannah was a baby. She gently patted Hannah's heart three times. "I love you, I love you, I love you."

Hannah's eyelids were already drooping.

"Goodnight, sweet Hannah," Reuben said, and now feeling at home with what was originally Rebecca's signature good-night gesture, touched his daughter's heart three times. "I love you, I love you, I love you."

They watched their daughter drift off to sleep again. Rebecca watched Hannah's easy breathing, strangely satisfied that all would be well.

Reuben waited for a moment, then whispered, "You ready?"

She took his hand, and, feeling surrounded again by the soft pulsing of the opalescent light, they found themselves in the yurt once more.

After chatting with the others in the yurt over a delicious meal, Reuben and Rebecca took a long walk together.

"Did you notice that coming *back* didn't take as long as traveling *to* Hannah?" Reuben remarked.

"I wondered if that was just me who felt that," said Rebecca. "I wonder if it's like so much here, where we are given a little bit at a time, and more slowly at first. Maybe after the first time, it speeds up as we get used to it."

Reuben nodded. "That makes sense."

"And did you feel kind of a soft pulsating sensation too?"

"Yes!" Reuben brightened. "You know what it reminded me of? You know how when you play with magnets, and when they face each other one way, they click together, but if you turn one around, you can feel this kind of soft force, pushing them apart? Well, it's not exactly like that, but ...."

"Yes!" Rebecca jumped in with the thought. "Like that, but with an easier flow."

They both paused, considering all these new ideas for a moment.

"Also," Rebecca mused, "when Lydia was just beginning to appear in Hannah's room, did you notice that she looked like those multicolored advanced beings that we met in the yurt? Then when she appeared fully, she looked the way we know her."

Reuben nodded, following her train of thought. "And did you notice ...." he began.

She nodded to urge him on. "Yes?"

"That *we* had the same colors around us when *we* were between places?" Reuben's eyes were bright with curiosity.

"Yes! I wonder what it all means. We'll have to ask Lydia and Thaddeus. Or maybe we should meet with the others at the yurt and ask them. I sure have a lot of questions." Rebecca paused. "Although, I feel, I don't know, kind of shy around those advanced beings."

"I know what you mean," agreed Reuben. "But there is nothing to be afraid of here. Maybe it would be a good way to see that that's true, by meeting with them."

They walked in silence for a while, and came to a small

lake. They followed a trail that went alongside the shore. It felt good to stretch their legs and enjoy the sounds of wind in the treetops, birdsong, and busy woodpeckers. They felt stronger now, and refreshed, and—amazingly—not at all worried about Hannah or anyone else. Yet they also felt a pull to return again. For them, it felt like several hours had passed. They agreed that their other questions could wait. Hannah came first.

They walked back to the yurt and found Lydia and Thaddeus eating watermelon at a table with Mahina and Eli.

"We'd like to go see Hannah again," Reuben told them.

Mahina nodded. "Yes, I can see that you're ready to go again."

"And, especially this time," Lydia said in an earnest but gentle tone, "follow your hearts. You will know what to do."

"Our love and support go with you," said Eli.

Rebecca and Reuben held hands. The thought of Hannah sent them in a colorful shimmer back to her bedroom, more quickly than the last time.

Again, Hannah didn't appear surprised to see her parents when she awoke. For her, they had just been there a moment ago. The three lay together, sometimes talking softly, but mostly relaxed in the quiet as Hannah drifted in and out of sleep. Rebecca and Reuben could hear Mike's muffled voice down the hall in Naomi and Fiona's room, reading them a bedtime story, punctuated with the girls' voices as they inserted questions and sound effects. Farther down the hall, they could hear dishes being washed. Kate, they knew, would be in the girls' room soon, to sing them a song as she always did. Rebecca and Reuben savored the normalcy with their baby, these moments of being together as if nothing had happened. Sometimes she woke and they sang songs together, but she soon drifted off again, and they simply watched her, listening to each soft inhale, each soft exhale. They reveled in the presence of their baby with her peaceful face, and their hearts were full.

Then the phone rang.

Rebecca sat up. She suddenly knew who would be on the phone, what Kate would soon face. How could she have forgotten that? She looked at Reuben. He sat up now, too, alert, remembering.

"What should we do?" Rebecca whispered to him. Hannah slept on.

"This is weird," Reuben scratched his beard the way he always had when trying to work out a problem. "It's not like we're reliving history. This is different. Last time we were not in this room, we were ...."

"I want to go to Kate. I want to help her with this. But I also want Hannah to have us here. I want to be here for her when this happens. But Kate's world is about to change, too. Oh, Reuben, what are we supposed to do?"

Reuben stared at his hands, dazed, trying to remember. "There is plenty of time," he said carefully. "All is well." He looked into Rebecca's face. "And whatever we do here," he spoke more quickly now, "whatever we talk about, however long it takes, it is the same as a *millisecond* on the earthly plane."

Rebecca became clear and focused. She touched both hands to her head. "We can relocate in an instant!"

Reuben met her eyes with equal intensity. "Yes!"

"I'll be right back!"

All Rebecca had to do was think of being near Kate, and instantly she found herself in the kitchen as Kate answered the phone.

"Hello?"

Rebecca moved closer to Kate.

"Yes, speaking."

She rested her hand on her niece's back.

"Yes, she's my aunt."

She waited.

"Excuse me?"

Rebecca stood behind Kate with her hands on her shoulders.

"What? No. She just went out to dinner with her husband. No, that can't be true. She's in a restaurant."

While Kate listened, Rebecca rubbed her back gently.

"Well ... uh. Just a minute." Kate groped for a pen, found a crumpled receipt to write on. She couldn't flatten it out. It flipped out of her hand onto the floor. She reached for it, but her toe kicked it first. "Just a minute," she said hastily and put the phone on the counter. She picked up the crumpled paper. It was too tiny to get open with her trembling fingers. She picked up the phone. "Just a minute," she said again, and put the phone down again. Rebecca watched, not knowing what to do. Kate turned around and around searching for something to write on. The Cooking with Kids cookbook lay on the counter. It had a blank page in the back. She tore it out and grabbed the phone again.

"Hello?" she asked doubtfully. "Yes, but ...." She couldn't go on. "Could you please tell me who this is again?"

Long pause. "But, are they okay?"

"Um ...." This couldn't be real. She cast a frantic look down the hall. She wanted Mike, but she didn't want the girls to ask what was going on when she didn't know herself. "So, uh .... So where do I need to go?"

Rebecca looked over Kate's shoulder at the address. Kate knew that area of town, which was a good thing, because her handwriting on the scrap of paper was impossible to make out.

"Okay. I'll be right there." Kate hung up the phone. She stood motionless for a moment, then sped down the hall to the girls' bedroom to get Mike.

Rebecca appeared in front of Reuben again. Hannah was sound asleep, and he was ready to go.

"Kate won't be able to concentrate. I have to get her there safely," she said to him.

"I know," he said. "Hannah will be fine here with Mike. I'm going to my boys."

Kate fumbled with her car keys. The officer said it had to be her. Mike would stay home with the girls. She turned the key in the ignition and shifted. Rebecca sat next to her.

"Katie," she whispered into Kate's ear. "It will be okay. I know it doesn't seem like it, but it will. I love you. You're stronger than you know."

Something told Rebecca to jump outside, behind Kate's car. She shooed away a raccoon. It was a good thing, because a moment later, Kate floored it and zoomed through the animal's former path, out into the street. Rebecca reappeared inside the car.

"Take it easy, Katie. I need you to take extra good care of yourself now. I love you. And now you're all that Hannah has. Speeding won't change what's happened. Slow down. I need you to be okay."

Kate slowed a bit and focused a little more. She tried without succeeding to make herself do a full stop at the sign. She drove on into the night, breathing short shallow breaths. Rebecca saw a motorcycle speeding around a corner ahead of them. "Slow down even more here, hon," she said into Kate's ear. Kate slowed enough to avoid the motorcycle, but her hands were shaking. She gripped the steering wheel harder and gulped for air.

Rebecca continued, "Remember our yoga class, Katie. Slowly, let your lungs take in more air, softly, deeply. Let it go when it's ready."

Kate took a deeper breath. She let it out more slowly this time, though her shoulders stayed high and stiff.

After another ten minutes, Kate saw it. She parked and approached the entrance to the funeral home, but stalled at the door.

Rebecca put a hand on Kate's back, just behind her heart. "You can do this. I need you to be strong and brave. You can do it, Katie. It really will be all right."

*   *   *

Jeffrey didn't speak. His jaw clenched, he nodded grimly at the officer, confirming that the body in front of them was, indeed, his and Ben's father.

Ben couldn't even nod. He and Jeffrey had just seen Reuben last night. The three of them had kicked a soccer ball around for an hour before they went for pizza. They one-upped each other with stories about the most impressive soccer matches they'd ever seen. This body with blood on his clothes was a stranger. It couldn't possibly be their dad. Someone had made a terrible mistake. Ben stood frozen to the floor, glanced at his dad's too-still, discolored face, then quickly away, then back, then away again. His nose plugged up; breathing through his mouth wasn't much easier. He felt feverish. Nauseated. Paralyzed.

Finally, with a hoarse, "Let's go," Jeffrey put his hand on the back of Ben's neck and steered him out the door.

In the green-tiled back hallway, Ben stopped again and turned to Jeffrey. They embraced.

Two attendants walked quietly around them, allowing for the silence that grief requires.

If Ben and Jeffrey had realized that Reuben was there too, his arms around them both, they would have seen the tears he shed for his boys, wishing he could heal their pain. They would have known he had been with them from Ben's house to Jeffrey's, and then to the funeral home. They would have known that he kept them focused on the road. And they would have understood why, rather than their usual brief hugs, they held on to each other tightly for several minutes, feeling—in spite of their pain—comforted and unwilling to let go.

*   *   *

Before Mike and Kate returned home, Rebecca and Reuben sat beside Hannah on the bed once again as she slept.

A door on the other side of the house closed. Voices arose in the living room. Mike and Kate were home. Muffled voices, mostly Mike's and their neighbor, Lorraine's, in the living room. Then Kate's staggering footsteps into Naomi and Fiona's room. Rebecca vanished and reappeared in the girls' room in time to see Mike still supporting Kate as she kissed their sleeping daughters and adjusted their covers. She lingered another moment, savoring the sight of her girls, saying a silent prayer over them. Then she spun around and headed for Hannah, Mike following closely behind.

Hannah was asleep when Kate and Mike entered. Rebecca and Reuben stepped aside as Kate gently picked up their baby and sat in the rocker, holding her, warm with sleep, to her chest. Kate began to cry in earnest now. Tears poured down her cheeks as she rocked Hannah.

Mike knelt beside the rocker and put his arms around Kate and Hannah. Kate squeezed Hannah closer and wept. She stroked her brown curls and kissed her head. She leaned back and closed her flooding eyes in pain.

Rebecca and Reuben watched Kate and Mike with their arms around Hannah, and knew they had done all they could for tonight. They focused on the soft pulsating and warm swirls of light and acquiesced. The bedroom faded from view, and they felt themselves drifting easily into much-needed rest, she in her now-familiar soft quilt, he in his hammock in the sun. In their individual spaces, they sensed more healing touch and fell easily into a deep nourishing sleep.

*   *   *

Rebecca awoke. Soft colors blurred together all around her, providing warmth and gently kneading her muscles Once again, she heard—or sensed—the soft humming she'd felt when she'd first arrived here. She couldn't make out a tune, but it wasn't monotonous either. She felt safe and secure, and uplifted. On the fringes of her mind, she knew she had just left Hannah, and she longed to comfort Kate, but even as she thought of this, she knew that she didn't need to worry.

At the same time, she realized that Reuben was nowhere in sight, and she knew that he, too, was resting and re-acclimating somewhere, and she let go of any need to think further for now. She let herself ease back into sleep.

The next time she awoke, she found herself lying comfortably on a beach towel on warm sand. She could hear waves breaking nearby. She stretched and sat up, chuckling. "Sheesh!" she said aloud. "You never know where you're going to wake up next around here." Her skin felt gently toasted from the sun. She hadn't been to the beach in ages. With a new surge of energy, she stood and walked to the water. On the wet firm sand, chilly waves ambushed her ankles, swirling foam around them, making her gasp and laugh. She turned to survey the beach in both directions. She saw Lydia, slim and trim in a blue one-piece swimsuit and wearing a ponytail, jogging easily down the beach toward her. She appeared to be in her thirties this time, but Rebecca recognized her easily.

"You did a beautiful job, dear," Lydia said as she drew near. She stopped in front of Rebecca and smiled. "How do you feel?"

Rebecca thought for a minute. "It's complicated, isn't it? I feel peaceful about, well, everything. But I also know that I want to go back. I feel … incomplete about it so far."

"Yes, I know what you mean."

Rebecca brightened, "Lydia, I'm so happy that Hannah can see us!" She grinned at Lydia, who beamed back at her. "I think that makes it easier for Reuben and me to adjust to all of these changes. It's hard, though, that Mike and Kate seemed to have no idea we were there. Could that be because they were so sad?"

"It could be," Lydia said. Though it is rare when any adult can see us. I guess you'll find out over time."

"It did seem like maybe Kate might have heard a *little* of what I was saying to her in the car; I'm not sure. Anyway, I'm eager to go back," Rebecca said. "And yet I feel content, too. It's hard to explain. There really is plenty of time, isn't there?"

Lydia nodded and gestured toward a large rock. They sat and watched the waves for a long time before Lydia asked, "Are you ready to change gears for a little while? There's someone who wants to talk with you."

"Okay," Rebecca said. "Sure."

"I'll stay with you as long as you want me to," Lydia assured her. She stood and led Rebecca up the beach for a few minutes, until they reached a level area with three Adirondack chairs. In one, a woman sat, wearing sunset-print luau pants and an orange tank top. Her shoulder-length layered hair was brown with some gray streaks. Rebecca didn't recognize her until she got closer and looked more carefully at the woman's face.

"Mother?"

Rebecca had always addressed her mother formally, even though this felt awkward to her. "Mom" had never been a name that seemed to fit their relationship. Rebecca had never felt close to her mother, and, in fact, had avoided her whenever possible. But now she felt safe enough to be curious.

Rebecca's mother stood, hesitated, and then stepped forward to greet Rebecca.

Lydia stepped in to bridge any potential awkwardness. "Hello, Betty," she said easily to Rebecca's mother, and stood next to her, putting her arm around Betty's tanned shoulders. She reached her other arm around Rebecca's waist, pulling her close, offering Rebecca extra reassurance. Rebecca let herself be held by Lydia while she surveyed her mother. She had changed drastically from the way Rebecca remembered her. Back then, she had worn her hair in a bouffant (always colored in later years to cover any gray) along with high heels and a belted-in dress, like those worn by "perfect" housewives and mothers on old TV shows. She had always moved stiffly with a joyless smile, eyes darting, monitoring, evaluating. Yet when company came, her voice became carefree, quick to joke. Now, in addition to her new tropical capris and natural hair, her face no longer had deep lines. She had a slight flush to her cheeks, her shoulders seemed less severe, her whole body moved more freely. However, she paused for a moment before speaking.

"Rebecca," she finally said, and reached out her free arm to touch Rebecca's arm.

"Hello, Mother," Rebecca said tentatively.

"I know it must be strange to see me like this. I thought about going back to my old look, just so that you would recognize me. But," she shrugged," I didn't want you to see me as I used to be. That's not me anymore. To tell you the truth, it never really was me. Besides, lately I've been going to Hawaii and walking in the rain. When my hair gets wet, I can just shake it out and it dries just the way I like it."

Rebecca didn't know what to say to this, so she just gave her a puzzled smile.

Her mother continued. "I have been empathizing with you since I got here several years ago. And I have learned a great deal about myself, too, since I arrived here and began my explorations. I've been eager to talk with you."

Even though this was probably the strangest thing that had happened here so far, Rebecca thought about the healing she experienced when she first arrived. If it hadn't been for that, she would have felt the roughness of the emotional calluses that had formed inside her over so many years. She probably would be walking away right now. But since her fear and a great deal of pain had been removed, she realized that, miraculously, she could have this conversation. Fortified by Lydia's arm around her, she spoke more clearly to her mother. "I'd like that," she said, nodding, already feeling more relaxed.

Her mother led them to the three chairs, and they sat. She gazed at the scenery for a moment. "Look at this beautiful ocean," she said to them. "I never lose my fascination for the magic and power, the gentleness and joy it brings."

They watched the waves crash for a few minutes. Rebecca let herself enjoy the fresh seaweed aroma. She found herself more comfortable and confident than she'd ever felt with her mother before. But even here she didn't feel exactly *friendly* toward her mother, just at ease. Now she knew that she'd be fine, no matter what was said.

"Rebecca, I ...." her mother began.

"It's okay," she told her mother.

Betty seemed to relax a little. "Rebecca, I went back and explored how life was for you all those years. It was the first time I really saw it, how ... how I let you down so many times."

Rebecca felt a surge of emotion in her heart for something that she needed but had long ago instructed herself was impossible.

"Your father," Betty paused and began again. "Your father has done some exploring, also, but he still has a long way to go before he will be ready to talk with you."

At the mention of her father, Rebecca remembered her childhood and the feeling of paralysis that often engulfed her whenever he was near. But now, instead of experiencing that same sensation, she knew it only as a memory, one that was outside of herself—like skimming a book about someone else. She could remember the details of it all, but it no longer carried the same weight inside her. She stopped to ponder this new point of view. Her mother seemed to understand, and waited.

Rebecca finally nodded at Betty and said, "I'm okay. Go ahead."

Betty waited respectfully for a moment. "You know, I think that most people expect that when they get here, they will be instantly healed and every problem will be fixed before they can blink. But really, it takes time to explore and learn, and, well, *grow into* the new life you are given. The wonderful thing is that you don't have to do this alone. I certainly needed guidance, and I had many kind souls who helped me in a variety of ways. It took me a long time for me to open up enough to trust even these loving people. I never was good at trusting anyone." She looked at Rebecca with compassion. "I believe that trust has always been hard for you, too. And perhaps that's why you became so independent." Betty waited another moment. "And I feel that the way I related to you probably caused your lack of trust."

Something profound moved in Rebecca's heart at this thought, but she couldn't grasp it enough to comment.

Her mother seemed to understand. She continued. "When someone leaves a life during which they hurt a child, they have much healing to do." She looked at Lydia. "Did you tell her about the healing temples yet?"

"No," Lydia said.

"Okay. Well, it seems appropriate that I be the one to tell you. When someone commits atrocities, it is because a split has occurred within them. A split is a chasm that gets created between the person they were meant to be and the person they behave as. The causes are complicated, but suffice it to say that the split must be healed before someone's progress can resume. People need help with that, so here we have healing temples. As you know, we *all* get healed of fear when we first arrive. When fear is gone, we are more willing to face the truth about other people's points of view. This is the exploration in empathy you have heard about.

"The more we empathize and ask for forgiveness, the more we are healed of the pain from our own lives, though not all at once, because if all pain disappears at once, we actually forget what pain is like, and then we are less able to empathize with any sense of the real truth of what someone else went through. And, of course, if you caused a great deal of pain for others, you stay in the healing temples for a much longer time. You must learn about the causes of the split, and this learning happens in tandem with the healing. Some find it surprising, but the people who *caused* pain to others require more healing than the people who *received* the pain." Betty looked at the ocean again. She seemed to be gathering strength to say the next thing. "I was in the healing temple for a very long time, because...." Betty hesitated. "My passivity was just as hurtful as your father's active abuse."

In all her life, it wouldn't have occurred to Rebecca that she could have a conversation about this with her mother. She couldn't believe this felt okay now. But her peaceful feeling remained, and she simply waited for Betty continue.

"I found forgiveness in the healing temples. It was profound—so *huge.* Well, that's not quite the word. But I don't know how else to describe it. From that experience, I felt forgiven, truly forgiven. As if I'd been carrying so much weight that I was never aware of before, but as soon as it was lifted, I laughed and cried in amazement. But the next step was to forgive myself, and I found that more challenging than forgiving others of anything. I hear that this is true for most people. That took me much longer than the first step. Finally, I found more of my burden being lifted, and I felt freer, to some degree. But I knew there was one more step. I knew that I needed to express my regrets to you. Sometimes—they tell me—it works to do this with people through dreams, but I haven't learned how to do that yet. I was just beginning to learn how, but now that you are here, I can talk directly with you instead.

"All this time, not having completion in this way left me with a task to do, but here, we are so surrounded by love, it doesn't burden us. Even when something is put on hold, we are still freer than we've ever been before; we just know there is a conversation we will need to have, eventually. We know we will be happier, freer, and lighter, when we can finally have it."

Rebecca looked at her mother, and her eyes brimmed with tears.

Betty scanned the horizon and let the sea air caress her face for a moment. "I hope this doesn't feel too invasive, but I've watched you for the past couple of years with your baby, Hannah."

Rebecca nodded again.

"I'm deeply touched at what a loving mother you are, Rebecca," Betty said. "She's a wonderful girl, truly happy, and it's clear that she knows that you and Reuben love her. You did that on your own. I can't take any credit for how you learned to be so nurturing. You should be proud of that, of parenting in a different way."

Rebecca opened her mouth, but she didn't know what to say.

"I also want to tell you … oh gosh, I hope I'm not piling on too much in one visit," Betty smiled tentatively at her daughter, her eyes welling. "I'm so relieved to get to tell you all this in person."

Rebecca felt a bit disoriented, but wanted to hear more. "It's okay," she said. "Go on."

"Well, just as you have visited Hannah, I visited you a number of times over the years. You were teaching up north, in Yonah River, when I died, and I know now, after empathizing with you, that you were feeling isolated from the rest of the family. After I got here, I realized how much I wanted to make up for not appreciating your uniqueness and for not supporting the excellent choices you made in your life. Sometimes I talked to you when you were asleep, other times when you were awake, driving, or cooking usually. And—I hope you don't mind! I was with you when you found out you were pregnant. I sat with you in the garden as you sorted through your feelings while you pulled weeds."

Rebecca sat up straighter, "Wait a minute." She tilted her head for a moment and peered at her mother. "Wait! When I was in the garden that day, I saw something. I remember that now. It was only for an instant, but it happened twice. The glints of light that I saw in my garden? I'd forgotten all about that! But *now* the memory is so clear in my mind! That was *you*?"

Betty and Lydia both smiled at Rebecca. "Ah, you always were very perceptive," Lydia laughed appreciatively.

"Yes, I was there," Betty confirmed. "I wasn't sure if you'd noticed. Your neighbor's cat saw me, though. Do you remember that?"

Rebecca laughed. "Oh, I forgot about Nutmeg! Yes, I do remember now, that he was acting kind of silly that day. But with a cat, it's never easy to tell why they do anything."

"True," laughed Betty. "Although the second time you saw something, he was distracted with a jasmine tendril. I guess that was more interesting to him than I was." She laughed again.

"Oh, I remember that, too. I was starting to think that stress was making me see things."

"Yes, that's why we try to be discreet with our visits. We don't want anyone to worry unnecessarily."

Rebecca nodded. "That makes sense."

"I also tried to comfort you when you were scared and talking with Reuben about whether or not Hannah would be born healthy, though I don't know how much help actually came through. Though I must say that Reuben did a fine job of being there for you. He's a good man."

Rebecca smiled at the thought of Reuben, and her heart filled with wonder at her mother's heartfelt words.

"And," Betty's expression became more serious. "Many times while you were pregnant, I came and sang to you. I guess I wanted to make up for never singing to you when you were young. I don't know why, but I always sang 'Goodnight, My Dear One,' and dared to hope that you might hear. It was hard for me to tell. But when you started singing the same song to Hannah, I knew that you really had heard me at least on some level."

Rebecca, her mouth open, looked to Lydia for confirmation.

"Yes, my dearest, it's true. Your mother has been trying to make things right for a long time." Lydia squeezed Rebecca's hand.

"So *that's* how I knew the words to the song?" Rebecca wondered.

"That's right," Lydia answered her.

"Rebecca, my daughter," Betty spoke more softly. "Your father will talk with you when he is ready. He and I have talked about our relationship, which is between us, but I *can* tell you that he feels a great deal of pain about his violent behavior toward you. You took the brunt of it, and he is working that out, with help. I think it is only right that I tell you that much. But the rest is his story to share with you. Meanwhile, I need to tell you how sorry I am that I stood by. That I didn't step in and protect you when he became violent. My choice to not intervene was a betrayal that no child should ever experience." Betty's voice cracked, but she continued. "I should have advocated for you. I should have done whatever it took to protect you. When I came here, the fog cleared from my mind and heart, and I saw for the first time how it felt to you every day of your growing up, how selfish I was to protect myself instead of you. If I could do it again, I would have given my life to prevent just one attack on you. But I can't go back. All I can do now is apologize and ask you to forgive me."

Rebecca's astonishment grew at these revelations that she had never expected to hear. Now Betty had stopped talking and waited quietly with tears in her eyes. It dawned on Rebecca that she had never seen her mother cry before. And now she saw that her mother had had pain in her life that Rebecca had been oblivious to. Finally, she found her voice.

"I forgive you," she said softly. She reached out and touched her mother's arm.

"Thank you," her mother whispered.

"You were trying to survive in the marriage," Rebecca realized aloud.

"That is how I saw it then, but it was wrong, nonetheless."

"You were scared, too."

"I should have been braver for you. You were my innocent child."

They sat in silence for a moment. Then her mother continued.

"There is something else," she said. "You will learn about this when you do your own exploration in empathy, but I want to tell you this much. I don't know if you can remember this part. You were so young when your father began to single you out. So, while I allowed your father to hit you, I took the moments I could when he was not around to show special kindnesses to you. I gave you extra hugs, hoping that would make up for the pain. But that was when you were small. Over time, I weakened and became more calloused.

"However, in many ways, even though your father didn't hit your sister, Martha, nearly as often as he hit you—and, as I said, you and he will explore that mystery together—I didn't provide any nurturing to Martha at all. As little as I gave you, I gave her even less. And she suffered for it. I tried to visit her and make it up to her after I arrived here, and I sang to her many times as well. But unlike you, she was not able to hear me. And so she continues to suffer. When you begin your exploration, you will see this. And perhaps then, you will understand why she was always so critical of you, even from a young age. Sometimes anger is caused by fear, but often, as in Martha's case, it is caused by pain. When you come to understand that, it will help you to heal the pain in your own heart about her."

Now Rebecca remembered, vaguely, that long ago, her mother *had* cuddled her. She remembered this for a moment, tracking it through time, and saw those hugs fade away by the time she was seven or eight. Had her mother really never hugged Martha back then? Ever? As she absorbed this strange new idea, she felt a different kind of sadness well up from deep inside her. She knew the pain of being judged and rejected by Martha, and of not being protected by her mother. Yet here sat a miracle, right across from her. Something she had never dreamed would happen.

The enormity of it washed over her. The healing that she had experienced when she first arrived had done a lot, but this was a different layer. She noticed Lydia nearby, ready to comfort, but Rebecca knew she needed to let this emerge on her own. Then she found herself standing and hugging her mother. An odd sensation it was, to hold her mother close, when she had never before wanted to do such a thing. Always, she had stiffened at merely touching shoulders if they had posed for family photographs. But now she felt lighter, safer, and reassured. Now she leaned into her mother, who, Rebecca noticed for the first time, was warm and pliant, a comforting body to sink into, resting her head on her mother's shoulder. And now her tears fell onto her mother's tank top, and her mother's tears ran onto Rebecca's hair. Betty kissed her head as they held each other closer.

Rebecca stood in Naomi and Fiona's bedroom that was now also Hannah's. She smiled at how Kate and Mike had rearranged the room with the girls' three beds side by side with no space between, Hannah's in the middle to keep her from rolling out. The guest bedroom next to this one could have been made into a room for Hannah, but Naomi and Fiona were eager to have her close by, and Kate and Mike felt that it was best for Hannah.

Next week, Kate and Mike would sign the adoption papers. They had agreed to Reuben and Rebecca's request that night after dinner—before Hannah was born—to be her legal guardians, should anything happen to Reuben and Rebecca. They had never dreamed that they would need to act on this promise.

Now that Hannah roomed with Naomi and Fiona, Rebecca and Reuben visited earlier in the evenings, after Mike or Kate tucked her in, but before Naomi and Fiona came to bed. They weren't sure if the older girls would be able to see them or not, and they decided not to complicate things right now with the possibility of them telling their parents that they could see Rebecca and Reuben or else that Hannah was talking to the air. Hannah seemed to view their presence with no surprise. They believed that even if she mentioned them, it would not seem that unusual to anyone, since lately she'd not only been talking to her stuffed animals, but had been creating imaginary friends in her games. And they were pretty sure that no one would be surprised if she "imagined" Rebecca and Reuben visiting her.

Tonight Rebecca lay next to Hannah, snuggling with her as they sang, "Great big stars, way up yonder," a favorite of

Hannah's that Rebecca had taught her not long ago. Hannah used to wiggle her fingers at the glow-in-the-dark stars on the ceiling above Hannah's bed. Now, Kate had placed stars above her new bed, and familiar stuffed animals and books surrounded her.

"Ah, my dear one, it's time for you to sleep." And time for me to go, Rebecca thought, as she felt the now-familiar swirl of warm colors that called her back to where she belonged. "Always remember how much I love you. My love surrounds you, near and far; love surrounds you, now and always," she sang softly. With her palm, she touched Hannah's heart three times, the way she always had. "I love you, I love you, I love you," she said softly. Hannah looked straight at her and smiled; then gradually, her lids drooped and closed. As she listened to Hannah's breathing become soft and rhythmic, Rebecca acquiesced to the warm pulsation and soft colors, and blew her daughter a kiss.

Rebecca and Reuben sat on a picnic blanket by a stream, eating their favorite mocha chip ice cream as they told each other about their latest visits and conversations.

"How are the boys doing?"

"They're okay. I think they're still in shock, but the good thing is that they are spending more time together. I'm grateful for that. I watch Jeffrey when he's alone in his apartment, and he slams doors a lot. He grinds his teeth sometimes in his sleep, too. I talk to him pretty often. I've experimented while he's awake *and* when he sleeps, but I think his logical brain keeps him from hearing me in either case."

Rebecca considered this. "Maybe that will change over time," she said hopefully.

Reuben nodded while they watched a bird peck at the dirt near the shore of the stream. "But sometimes I think Ben hears me. Sometimes he seems to relax more when I talk to him while he sleeps. I sure hope so. I hate to see him in pain. But guess what? There's a girl who is interested in him."

"Ooh! What's she like?"

"They've been in a couple of art classes together at the community college. He had mentioned her to me before, but he never made it sound like there was anything going on beyond being acquainted. Maybe he just didn't feel certain enough to say so, but watching them, I think there's more. They mostly eat out and take walks. I like her. She listens when he talks about me. And she can make him laugh. I love seeing that."

"Oh, I'm glad. He needs that."

"Yeah. I feel relieved that he's relaxing and seeing fresh possibilities in life."

Reuben's dogs, Lucy, Bullwinkle, and Rocky, rolled in the grass nearby with some other dogs, frequently jumping up for wild chases around the trees before collapsing into laughter in the grass again. At a nearby picnic table, a group of women sat chatting over rhubarb pie. In the middle of the table sat Gertrude, Rebecca's guinea pig, who much preferred to discuss literature with the women at the table than to romp with the dogs, even though she acknowledged cheerily enough that they were quite adorable.

Reuben watched his dogs for a minute, chuckling, and then continued. "I've taken some time to just relax with Thaddeus, and that's been fun. We've been trout fishing."

"Really? You can fish in heaven? How does *that* work?"

"I wondered about that, too." Reuben smiled. "You ever play tug of war with a dog?"

Rebecca gave him a sideways look.

"Well, it's like that. Sometimes you pull the fish out of the water, but sometimes *they* pull *you into* the water. It's a fun game for everyone. But just like anyone else, sometimes they're in the mood to play and sometimes they're not. And the new-arrival trout are hesitant to join in for a while, until they're sure that the end result here is not like it was on earth."

"Understandable."

"And sometimes the fish aren't there at all when we go looking for them. They leave the creek and go visit other bodies of water. They can relocate just the way we do. Did you know that?"

Rebecca just shook her head.

"I guess," Reuben speculated, "maybe trout who spent their whole lives in a mountain stream want to visit the Caribbean, or who knows where else?"

"Makes sense."

"Sometimes they leap out of the water for fun, and we try to grab them. Did you know that trout are ticklish?"

He watched Rebecca, his eyes sparkling, as she laughed.

"Anyway," he continued, "Thaddeus and I have gotten a bit philosophical lately, comparing new perspectives that I've been learning about."

"I've been pretty blown away by new perspectives myself,"

Rebecca commented, looking across the lawn at Gertrude.

One of the women got up from the table and strolled over to Rebecca and Reuben.

"Jewel!" Rebecca greeted her. "Reuben, this is Jewel Peabody, Martha's old neighbor."

"Hi, Jewel," Reuben held out his hand. "Glad to meet you."

"You too, Reuben." She shook his hand. "May I join you?"

"Please," Rebecca said. She and Reuben made a space for her. Rebecca had met her only once at Martha's house after their mother's memorial service. At that time, Jewel was almost ninety. Right now, Jewel looked about thirty. But Rebecca recognized her easily.

"I'll get right to the point," Jewel said kindly. "I hope you don't mind, but I'd love to share a little with you about your sister, Martha."

Rebecca felt herself become more serious than she had been all day, but curiosity prevailed. "My niece, Kate, told me that Martha cooked a lot of meals for you."

"She did, indeed. Dinner every evening. *Every evening!* In my last several years over there—I lived to be ninety-five, you know—I had many ailments, and the simplest things became very difficult for me. Your sister was one of the most kindhearted people I had ever known."

Rebecca glanced at Reuben.

Jewel observed the look and continued. "Yes, I know about the difficulties between you two. But I want you to know that there is another side of her. It meant the world to me to know that she was just a phone call away, and that she would check on me every day. Not only were the meals she cooked for me a kind gesture—and delicious—but they were a way of making the need to simply check on me less conspicuous. She let me keep my dignity. And she was so kind, never grudging. Always cheerful, and not in a fake way, either. I could feel that it really was from her heart. If it weren't for your sister, I probably would have had to move into a nursing home for those last years. My husband died at a young age, and both of my children died many years before me, you know." She shrugged and added, "That's what comes from me having great genes, but my kids inheriting my husband's less-than-perfect health genes."

"Wow," Reuben shook his head.

"Mm," she nodded at Reuben. "Anyway, I believe that Martha will be okay eventually. It's important for her to remember something that will cause her pain, but it will heal her in the end."

"There is so much I have to learn." Rebecca touched her heart. "This was good for me to hear. Thank you, Jewel."

"You're welcome, darlin'." She got up and squeezed Rebecca's shoulder. "Any time you want to talk, just holler." She turned to Reuben. "I'm so glad to meet you in person."

"You, too," Reuben said. "Thanks."

Jewel strolled away, her sandaled feet brushing through the green grass, the dogs dancing around her. "Hi, honey pies!" she greeted them. The dogs chatted happily with Jewel as they escorted her back to the picnic table.

"Whew!" Rebecca said to Reuben. "You know, this is the first time in years that I feel there could be some hope for Martha and me."

"This is interesting timing, too," Reuben commented, "since we're about to see her."

"I'm starting to think that maybe, besides forgiving people, maybe what we need to do is just let down our guard about people. I think all my life, because of our history, I just kind of braced myself whenever I was around Martha. Now I'm realizing that, hey, I've been healed of my fears. Maybe I don't have to brace myself anymore."

Reuben nodded, squinting as he listened.

"That sounds funny, in a way," she continued. "I mean, why would I worry about being safe around her when I'm here now? I guess it's just a reflex, an automatic thought. Even healing takes some getting used to, doesn't it?"

"Lots to learn," Reuben mused.

Rebecca resumed eating her ice cream, which was still just the right temperature and creamy texture. "I feel like there is a whole lot more to do besides our visits with Hannah, you know? And I'm getting excited about it. But right now, I am more curious about what today is going to be like. I mean, I never thought about observing my own memorial service!"

Reuben shook his head. "I know. Boggling." He took another spoonful of ice cream. "You know, one of my biggest concerns has been about my dad."

"I can imagine," Rebecca said. Reuben's dad was the only one of their parents still living. Reuben had expressed his sadness to Rebecca before. It felt unreasonable, unfair, for any parent to have to grieve the death of their child. He had chatted with Thaddeus about it just the other day.

"Well, yes, he's sad, of course," Thaddeus had said.

"But he'll be okay. It's all okay, Reuben. You'll see. He'll be all right. And he's got Hannah to visit. That'll keep him busy!" Thaddeus had winked, and had said, almost to himself, "Those little buggers sure can keep a guy jumping."

Reuben finished his last spoonful and looked at Rebecca. "You ready?"

"I am. Let's go."

The little chapel overflowed with friends and family. The afternoon air wafted softly into the open windows and doors, a welcome relief as people continued to arrive, crowd into the pews, stand in the outer aisles, and, finally, in the doorways, for the memorial service.

In a small room down the hall, Reuben and Rebecca found Jeffrey and Ben with Reuben's sister, Sarah, his brother, Jacob, and their dad, Thomas. Thomas sat next to Sarah and held her hand as he stared absently into the middle of the room.

"Dad," Reuben said softly. He stood next to him, not sure what to do. His dad looked more tired than Reuben had ever seen him.

Seeing his sister and brother, Reuben shook his head, feeling a wave of regret for how seldom they had visited each other. He went over to Sarah and looked into her face. Her hair was the same dark brown as his, but she had only slight waves, worn in a shoulder-length cut. He hugged her, then moved behind her and their dad, and put a hand on each of their shoulders.

Ben had been talking softly, and now he heaved a shaky sigh. "I don't know if I can do this," his voice quavered.

Sarah, who had been focusing on her dad, turned to Ben. "Ben, for one thing, your dad loved you and was so proud of you. But another thing I know for a fact: He's right here, still loving you. That will never stop, and he will come alongside you whenever you need him most." Sarah stopped for a minute, watching dubious faces looking back at her. "I know. I can't believe I just said that. It is so unlike me to think that way. But suddenly, I just knew it. And I think it's true for all of us. He's here. He loves us. Present tense. *Ongoing*." She shook her head, as if adjusting to these new ideas that were suddenly in her mind, but continuing in a full, calm, confident voice. "Ben, I know that this is true. And I think that your dad wants you to know that you're stronger than you think. And I think that he's going to get you through this today." She patted her dad's hand.

Reuben gave his sister a kiss on her cheek. "Thank you," he whispered. Then he stood behind his father and rubbed his back.

His dad sat up straighter. "It'll be okay," he said. They all looked at him. This was the first thing he'd said since they had arrived at the chapel. "I don't know how I can know that, not with how terrible this is, but somehow I know it."

Sarah put her arm around her dad. "God I miss him," she managed to say. "I know that sounds crazy since we hardly ever visited or even talked on the phone, but I miss him terribly."

Jacob watched his sister while she talked. He was blinking

and looked awkward in his slacks and jacket. A piece of fuzz perched just above his temple in his dark brown hair, curly like Reuben's but cut closer. He had been sitting quietly, but now spoke in a hoarse voice. "You boys were always good sons to him. You spent lots of time with him." His voice became softer. "You can always feel proud about that." He stared at nothing in particular, and didn't say anything more.

Reuben sat next to him on the padded bench seat. He hugged his brother, whose eyes welled with tears, though he remained silent.

Everyone in the group seemed lost in their own thoughts for a few moments, until a soft knock at the door interrupted the quiet. The door opened a bit, and Susan, the minister who had officiated at Rebecca and Reuben's wedding, peeked in. "May I come in?" she asked.

"Yes. Yes, please!" Sarah held up an arm in welcome. Jeffrey stood up and held the door for her. He, too, had said very little since their arrival.

"Let's have a short visit before we start." Susan came in and sat next to Jeffrey as he returned to his place on the couch. "How is everyone doing right now? Are there any feelings you'd like to discuss before we begin the service? I know this is still a terrible shock. It's only been six days since we lost Rebecca and Reuben. It might not feel real yet."

Rebecca was aghast. "Only six days? Seriously?"

"Wow." Reuben shook his head. "I guess I knew that, vaguely, but it feels like much longer. I mean, *much* longer. Think of everything we've seen, everything we've learned. In some ways, it feels like *years*."

Rebecca agreed. "I can't believe it. And yet, I guess I can. And maybe I'm starting to get it, just a little bit, anyway, what Lydia means. I mean, just a few minutes ago …. Hmmm, how long was it *actually*? What does that even *mean* anymore? We were …." Rebecca shook her head, trying to sort her thoughts.

"I know," Reuben picked up the thought. "We were just eating ice cream. Why would we do that when we feel that there is so much to do? Except that I'm learning, too—gradually—that there really is plenty of time. That we will be able to do anything we want to. There is no rush. And maybe …. Hmm, maybe we do it *better* when we've taken time to relax between visits."

"Lydia says taking time between visits helps us to establish our intuitions more fully, which 'pays off in a pinch,' as she says." Rebecca smiled at the thought of her friend's expressions.

Reuben considered this. "Not long ago, I wouldn't have gotten that at all. But now it's making more sense to me. I wonder …."

A knock at the door brought them back to the discussion among Reuben's family. Susan opened the door to let in Martha, Brad, and Greg, followed by Kate and Mike with Hannah, Naomi, and Fiona. Rebecca's relatives had never met Reuben's siblings before. They found places to sit and talk for a few minutes. Then Susan said a prayer and led them down the hall to the chapel.

Rebecca and Reuben perched on the edge of the dais and surveyed the crowd. In the front row sat Reuben's dad, Sarah, Jacob, Jeffrey, and Ben. In the next, Martha sat with Brad on one side and Kate on the other. Hannah, Mike, Naomi, Fiona, and Greg filled up the rest of the row. A few rows back sat Ellen and Ann. Besides people that Rebecca and Reuben had been friends with for many years, both separately and together, they saw many coworkers as well as former and current students, including Gina and Carlos.

Reuben whispered to Rebecca, "I had no idea so many people would show up! I even see some parents of my students. I guess you can never really predict these things."

Rebecca nodded, but she gave him a mocking smirk. "Why are you whispering?" she asked in full voice.

Reuben laughed. "Oh, yeah!" and he added loudly, "I forgot!" and looked around at the lack of reaction.

"Couldn't resist teasing you about that," she laughed. "But you are right about the crowd. It's boggling."

Susan spoke a few words of welcome and said a prayer. Then she said, "The family will have a private scattering of the ashes tomorrow, up the coast. But today is a day to remember together, to celebrate the lives of two people we will always treasure in our hearts." She stood to the side while Mike read a poem.

Then Ellen came to the podium. She brushed auburn locks of hair from her face that had already freed themselves from her bun as she shared memories of her friendship with Rebecca that had started in preschool. She told about how, in junior high, they had cut class together (this caused some gasps and laughter among her students), talked late into the night during sleepovers at each other's houses, screened each other's latest heartthrob, laughed themselves silly, cried together, and could always count on each other for an honest answer.

"I feel pretty confident that she's in a good place right now. But ...." Ellen's next word caught in her throat. The room waited in silence for her. Those nearby could hear a quiet gulp. "But I don't ...." Her mouth contorted. Rebecca moved to Ellen's side as Ellen's voice rose in pitch. "I don't know what I'm going to do without her." Rebecca stood behind her with her arms around her, hugging her close with her head next to Ellen's. Ellen stood for another minute, allowing the tears to spill. Then she whispered, "I'm sorry, that's all I can say." She walked slowly down the three steps, shakily holding onto the railing. Ann met her partway up the steps (Rebecca read her determined expression as wanting to help Ellen and trying to save her own emotions for later) and walked her back to her seat.

Gina got up next with another student, who stood next to her for moral support. She said, "I never thought I would stand in front of all these people and say anything." She gave a half-laugh, while other students chuckled sympathetically, knowing how true this was about Gina's shyness. "But I wanted to share a poem by Mary Oliver that Ms. T gave to me one day when I felt discouraged. It's meant a lot to me ever since then." And she read the entire poem with a full confident voice.

"That's my girl," Rebecca beamed at Gina.

Mark got up next. He waited respectfully for a moment,

then shifted his stance and addressed the crowd. "Reuben and I taught together at the high school for twenty-seven years," he said. "But he was more than a coworker. He was my best friend. And I would be a failure as a best friend if I didn't tell about the time we went on a research trip in the Great Bear Rainforest of British Columbia one summer."

"Oh, no! He's not going to tell *that* story!" Reuben laughed and smacked his forehead.

Rebecca clapped her hands. "He *has* to tell it! It's one of his best!"

Reuben rolled his eyes in mock agony. "Yeah, I guess so." He listened to Mark tell the lead-in to the story.

"It's interesting, isn't it?" Reuben pondered aloud. "Did you ever wonder what people would say about you?"

Already the crowd was laughing as Mark got more animated, illustrating the story with his gestures.

"No, I guess I never gave it any thought," she mused. "Now I'm beginning to think I should have. I wonder what else we'll hear today."

Another uproarious laugh. Reuben paused for a moment, listening to his best friend. "Here comes the punch line."

Mark finished off his story. People hooted and wiped away tears of laughter while he waited. His face now serious, he said in a thicker, tighter voice, "I miss you, bud," and walked quickly back to his seat.

Reuben toasted his friend with an imaginary beer mug in his hand. "You'll be all right, guy," he croaked hoarsely. "I'll join you on some bike rides, okay?"

*   *   *

Kate stayed in her seat with Hannah snuggled in her arms, Naomi and Fiona next to her. She had brought plenty of stuffed animals for them to play with, and they often climbed into her lap or Mike's. She had so much in her heart that she wanted to say. But there was no way she could stand up and say it here. This was still too raw. Besides, how could you condense all that someone was to you in one short talk? It couldn't be done. She welcomed the distraction of having the girls to watch after. She had considered leaving them at home, having their neighbor, Lorraine, babysit. But after she and Mike talked with Susan, the minister, a few days ago, they decided that, even if the three girls didn't fully comprehend what was happening at this gathering, they would be surrounded by the community of Rebecca and Reuben's friends. Everyone would see Hannah as part of Kate and Mike's family now. A family of five, a family in pain who needed the support of a village.

No, she couldn't talk right now. Just being here was hard enough.

Hannah sat up and blinked at the podium. She smiled brightly at Rebecca and Reuben, and wiggled her fingers at them. To Kate, it looked like she'd made friends with Susan from afar.

*   *   *

Martha sat straight in her seat. She felt a migraine coming on. She fingered the stitches on the hem of her skirt as the others talked up front. She didn't know any of these people. Except for Ellen. She remembered her hanging around the house in high school. Sheesh, that girl would never go home. Those two were inseparable.

Now here were these students. *Just look at them.* Images of young people, inappropriately dressed, blurred in her vision, sprinkled with sparks of light stabbing at her eyes. How could Rebecca relate to them? Obviously, she manipulated everyone into thinking she was this great selfless person. *I'm hearing all these stories, and now, now I don't even know who she was. Now it's too late.* She felt a tremor in her neck, and her eyes stung. *All I saw was a kid sister who got her way with our mother all the time and left me out. I guess no one is aware of that. Am I the worst person in the world to be thinking about that at a time like this?*

And now, look at that baby. No one ever comments about how much she looks like Rebecca. Everyone comments that she has Reuben's hair, but that's nothing. Look at those intense eyes! How can I see her and not think of Rebecca? What am I going to do? From now on, she'll be there every time I visit Naomi and Fiona.

She watched as Ellen struggled up front to get her words out. *They both helped each other get through tough times? What kind of tough times did they have?*

Rebecca meant something to these people. What did I miss? How could they see her so differently than I did?

She heard a shaky gasp of air next to her as Brad continued to fight his tears. She scowled, though she tried to do it internally so she wouldn't make a scene. *I don't understand Brad, either. He left home when he turned eighteen and never looked back. What does he have to cry about? I'm the one who stayed through all the hard times. I'm the one who put up with Rebecca's teenage behavior. I'm the one who took care of our parents after the two of them left me to do it alone. My head is splitting. I have to go home*

*   *   *

Now students and teachers from Reuben's and Rebecca's schools stood in the outer aisles, creating a circle. Carlos started with the handheld microphone, telling how—thanks to Rebecca's encouragement—he had received a scholarship award and had already completed two years of college, the first in his family to go beyond high school. He passed the microphone to another student, who shared a story about the year Reuben coached soccer. Now many students and teachers stood with arms around each other, sharing memories of fiascoes in the biology lab, extra help after school, listening during a crisis, sometimes just one word of thanks. Some just passed the microphone along, some cried, some laughed, as they expressed their appreciation and grief together. Rebecca and Reuben felt surprised several times at who showed the most appreciation; often it was a student who had never seemed to care one bit. And they laughed and cried along with their students.

Reuben threw his arms open. "This is *great!*"

"Incredible," Rebecca murmured as she watched her students, the parents, the teachers.

Susan stood and entreated everyone to "… rally around Kate and Mike as they take Hannah into their family and raise her as their own with Naomi and Fiona. You can honor Rebecca and Reuben in this way." She ended with a prayer, and people filed out.

Brad stayed where he was, not yet ready to talk to anyone. After everyone was out of the chapel and on their way across the lawn to the reception hall, Susan came back in and touched him on the shoulder. "Stay as long as you need to. I'll be in my office." She tiptoed out.

Rebecca came and sat next to her big brother. "I love you, you big dork," she said, with one arm around him. "Don't worry about me, okay? Believe it or not, it's wonderful over here, and even though it might not feel like it right now, everything is going to be fine. Guess what? I talked with Mother! Can you believe that? She's really sorry about everything. She knows that doesn't change the past, but she helped me to understand some things. Do me a favor, okay? Will you check on Martha? I'm starting to figure out some things about her. I think she could use your support. Yeah, she's prickly all right. But give it a shot, okay big brother?"

Brad rubbed his face roughly, and gulped air. More tears fell.

"Hey, don't blame yourself. You tried, and then you had to take care of yourself. It was the right thing to do. Let go of that, okay?"

Brad had his elbows on his knees now, and was sobbing.

"I love you, big brother." She rubbed his shoulders, kissed his head, and leaned into him.

Reuben came in and stood by her. "Becca," he said quietly.

She sighed. "I know. It's too much at once. I just feel so bad for him."

"You can try again later."

"You're right." She rubbed Brad's shoulders once more before letting go.

In the reception hall, they mingled and listened to stories. They watched Hannah toddle after her new big sisters as they ran around the room, stopping for cookies at the refreshment table. Hannah stopped to smile at her parents. They blew her kisses, which she blew back. With so many people in the room, everyone thought she was blowing kisses to them, and they were charmed all the more.

Clouds of ash billowed in the wind from the two urns. Puffs of white sailed up quickly, as grainier bits swirled downward to the side of the foggy California coastal cliff. Some made it to the waves crashing on the rocks below; some rested, at least for now, on mugwort (*Artimisia douglasiana*, Rebecca smiled as she remembered), lupines, rosemary, wild iris, angelica, sea thrift, shore pines, and cypress, all staunchly rooted among large and small rocks.

Jeffrey and Ben, Kate, Mike, Brad, Martha, Sarah, Jacob, Mark, and Ellen stood on Rebecca and Reuben's favorite hiking trail, near their favorite campground.

"I thought I would feel something about seeing crumbly bits of my body get blown away by the wind. But it's Jeffrey and Ben that are getting to me," Reuben said as he watched his sons. A tear slid down Ben's cheek as Jeffrey stood next to him, jaw clenched.

Rebecca nodded silently, watching her sister and brother and Kate.

Urns now empty, save a fine dust that would remain, the small group of family and friends stood quietly, some arm in arm, reflecting.

*   *   *

This was the last ceremony they had to go through, and Martha felt relieved. She stood behind Kate with her hands on her shoulders. Her daughter, Kate—now so grown and maternal herself. Martha softly gathered Kate's hair into a ponytail, letting it go, brushing strands from her face, gathering again.

*   *   *

Kate said nothing, only hugged Rebecca's urn to her and

tried to take comfort in the flowering rosemary, the oat grass, the gulls above, that Rebecca would have loved. She felt her aunt's absence as a hollow pain in her stomach. Her throat tightened and her shoulders ached.

*   *   *

Brad stood alone at the edge of the cliffs, watching the water that now carried his baby sister's ashes as it swirled around the rocks. Ben sat on a rock overlooking the cliffs. Jeffrey picked at the shrubbery, seeming to examine each leaf. Ellen, Ann, Mark, and others stood off to the sides, staring at the view, lost in their own thoughts.

Gradually, the group resumed their quiet hike along the trail, remembering, chatting.

"Wow," Rebecca whispered as she watched them walk away. Then she and Reuben felt the now-familiar soft pulsating as they shifted from earth's atmosphere back to heaven.

*   *   *

The last of the guests finally gone, Martha closed the full dishwasher and started on the serving dishes and pots. She wore an apron over the jeans and sweater that she had worn on the hike. Soapsuds flew onto the black granite countertops and checkered floor, as well as her apron.

Brad came in with three more glasses from the living room. "Can I dry?" he asked.

"I'm almost done." The edge to Martha's voice was blurred by exhaustion.

Brad looked around. "I thought Isabelle was in here with you."

"She had to go home. She has to get up early in the morning for work."

"I'm sorry; I didn't realize you were doing this alone."

"You've been no help at all this whole time. All you've done since you got here was sit around and cry. Once again, you left everything to me."

Brad felt his heart pound. He stood frozen for a moment, mouth open, staring at Martha. "Our *sister* just died!" he finally choked out. "Don't you have any feeling about that at all? Have you shed one tear for her?"

"Someone's got to feed this crowd." Martha grabbed her steel wool and scrubbed at the beef and vegetable residue on the large soup pot. "Kate has too much on her plate with suddenly having a third child."

Brad stepped over to the sink. "Wait. Stop. I'll do the rest of the dishes. Let's sit and talk for a minute."

Martha kept scrubbing. "I'll do it," she said grimly.

Part of Brad wanted very much to leave. But tugging at the back of his mind was a feeling that there was more that needed to happen right now, more that he needed to see about Martha that he hadn't seen before. He wasn't sure exactly what, but the feeling nagged at him. "Martha," he finally said aloud. "I'm leaving tomorrow. Can we please talk?"

"I have to get these dishes washed." She bent her head low and scrubbed harder.

Brad grabbed his head with both hands. "Martha, what the *hell* is so important about washing dishes? They'll *wait* for you! *Please!* Talk to me!"

Martha stopped scrubbing, rested her wrists on the sink's edge, and heaved an angry sigh, her attention locked on the sudsy pot.

Brad tried again. "I know this is terrible timing, what with everything that's happened with Greg too. I can't begin to imagine how painful that's been for you, feeling betrayed like that, and having to go through it more than once the past couple of years. I had no idea that any of that was going on. It would be devastating for anyone. I would never bring up this stuff about Rebecca with you right now, but I'm leaving tomorrow. And we *have* to talk. We *have* to. Please, Martha."

Martha held her ground, gripping the edge of the sink.

"Come on. I'll do it after we talk. I promise." He picked up the bottle of dish soap, poured some in the pot, and filled the rest with water. "See? I'm even soaking it."

Martha threw the steel wool into the sink and peeled off her rubber gloves. She turned to him, leaning against the sudsy counter. "Make it quick."

"Excellent. Now come over here. You want another glass of wine?" He didn't wait for an answer. He found her glass on the windowsill above the sink and took it into the dining room where partly full wine bottles stood. "Zin?"

Martha's shoulders slumped in resignation. She nodded. Brad poured her a glass. She'd probably already had plenty to drink tonight, he thought, but he had to get her to stop scrubbing and talk to him. He glanced around for another clean glass, but found none. Hastily, he grabbed a clean coffee mug next to the air pot on the sidepiece, and poured some chardonnay for himself. He led her into the living room. Martha sat. Brad pulled a nearby chair closer to her. He found coasters and placed them on the side table for Martha's sake, along with the wine bottles for refills. He faced her, holding his mug of wine in both hands. "Martha ...."

"Don't get on my case for not crying," she interrupted in a thick voice. Martha focused on rubbing a smudge from her wine glass. "You've done enough crying for both of us." She finally looked at him and her pitch rose. "I don't understand that either. Why do you care so much? You left us the first chance you had, and you've hardly come back since. You ...."

"Martha, I've been the worst brother in the world. I know that. I'm sorry. I mean it. I'm really, *really* sorry." Brad set his mug down carefully on a coaster and reached out to take her free hand, but she pulled it away. He forged on. "But, well, Rebecca and I have kept in touch in recent years. You never seemed to want to. So, I didn't press. But now I'm sorry I didn't."

"You contacted her and not me?" Martha frowned at him.

"I did contact you, about ten years ago; I tried a few times, but you weren't exactly welcoming."

Martha looked out the window.

"Martha, I just finally gave up. I'm sorry." He waited for a reply, but none came. "The thing is, I want to tell you now what I've learned. It doesn't repair the past at all. I know that. But maybe it will help us both understand each other. Maybe we don't have to keep feeling so bad if we can just understand things a little better."

Martha continued to stare out the window.

"Okay. I'm just going to talk to you, and I hope you'll listen." Brad took a deep breath and let it out through his nose. "There was a lot of pain in our house growing up, Martha. I know you know that, but we've never talked about it. Dad was angry all the time, and hit us all, and our mother never did one thing about it. There was nothing any of us could do. My way of coping was to sign up for every sport I could possibly qualify for. I stayed away. It worked for me. But it *didn't* work for you and Rebecca."

Martha flinched. She swallowed hard and pressed her lips together.

"Especially Rebecca," he added.

Martha swung around and glared at Brad. "You think that's how it was? *Poor* Rebecca? *That's* what you think?" She looked like she was preparing to yell louder, but a loud sob escaped, which made her swear. She put down her wine glass, took a deep breath, and leaned forward with her head in her hands before exhaling loudly.

"Yes, as a matter of fact, I do. You know that he hit Rebecca way more than he hit us. I don't understand that, but that's what happened. There was something about her that set him off. She didn't have to say or do anything much at all, and he'd be on her case about everything, yelling and swinging. And all our mother could do was act as prim and proper as she knew how, like she believed it would all just not be true if only she could keep a tidy house and follow all the etiquette books. As if it was okay—even the wisest course—to ignore Rebecca's crying." Brad's throat tightened around these last words. He said hoarsely, "It still makes me feel like throwing up when I think about it." He paused. "Something I learned while I was in therapy …."

Martha threw both hands up in disgust then crossed her arms.

Brad persisted. "Something I learned is that kids in abusive families tend to choose one of two strategies: they either hyper-bond with each other or they each isolate themselves in their own protective bubble." Martha's eyes finally met his. "It's pretty obvious which survival strategy the three of us chose."

Martha picked up her wine glass again and took another swallow. She looked around the room, as if searching for something. "Our mother spoiled Rebecca to death, and she never gave me the time of day. Rebecca manipulated her. She …."

"Martha, he beat the crap out of her. I mean, he hit us all, but a few years ago, she described some situations to me that I never knew had happened because I wasn't home."

"Well, I see that she manipulated you too," her voice wobbled.

"She had no reason to exaggerate, Martha. She had nothing to gain by telling about these things after all these years, after our parents were both gone. I may never understand why our dad hated Rebecca so much, and while I can take some guesses about our mother's passive silence, it doesn't excuse it. Rebecca went through serious therapy to get past that. She and I talked a few years ago. She found a lot of healing about our parents' behavior, but what she wanted more than anything, that she was never able to achieve, was a better relationship with you. She told me that she tried to explain to you what she had learned, but you wouldn't listen. That's why she gave up and stayed away from family events and moved away from here for so long. It was too frustrating, too painful to keep trying."

Martha put her glass down and stood. "She ...." she began. "She ...."

Martha collapsed back into her armchair, grabbing firmly onto the sides. Then she flailed her arms out, and Brad wondered what she was reaching for. Stunned for a moment, he now leaped forward and grabbed her hands. He sat on the ottoman in front of her, and leaned closer.

She pulled her hands from his.

Oh, no, he thought. *I've done too much.*

But instead of the disaster that he anticipated, Martha put her hands on his arms, then—to his surprise—she latched onto his shoulders, threw herself against him with her arms around him, and heaved a loud tearless sob.

Brad held her and waited, not moving, for fear he'd disrupt whatever was happening.

After a few moments, she disentangled herself from him, but kept her hands on his arms. She hung her head and sighed heavily.

"I'm so exhausted," she said, barely loud enough for him to hear.

"I know. And you have reason to be," he said softly, trying to stay passive.

They sat in silence.

Eventually she looked at him. Her face had softened, though traces of confused furrows remained. "I think I need to be alone for a while. To think about things."

"Okay," he said. Then he added cautiously, "My flight leaves tomorrow afternoon. Can I come by before that?"

"I'm not sure. I just don't know. I don't know anything," she slurred. She kept her hands on his arms.

"I could change my flight. I could stay longer."

"No. I mean ... I don't know. I don't think so."

"How about if I call you in the morning?"

"Okay." She sighed again.

Brad got up and kissed her head. Martha stood up, as if awakening, trudged into the kitchen, and put her rubber gloves back on. She dumped the soapy water out of the pot and grabbed the steel scrubber.

Brad tripped after her. "Will you please let me do that? I promised you I would."

"No, I need to do this," she said, with more firmness in her voice. "Really. It helps me." She saw his skeptical face. "*Really*," she repeated, now giving him her more customary glare.

"Okay," he put his hands up in surrender. "I'll call you in the morning."

Martha nodded.

Brad let himself out the kitchen door.

*　　　　*　　　　*

Martha scrubbed steadily at the pot, which was already clean. Nevertheless, she scrubbed. Her face felt hot, and her eyes burned. Her throat tightened, and she could feel her cheeks and mouth contorting. But no. She would not cry.

She rinsed the pot and placed it in the drainer. She grabbed a serving dish, squirted soap into it, chose a nylon scrubber, added hot water, and kept working.

*   *   *

Rebecca watched Brad close Martha's door. She brushed away her tears and said to Lydia, "How is it that you can still cry in heaven? How can it be that I'm here and I can cry, but Martha seems incapable? None of this is what I would have imagined."

"That's the point." Lydia touched Rebecca's wet cheek. "Here, you have more courage, so it is easier to feel complete emotion. When fear is gone, we shed the belief that something disastrous could happen if we allowed our emotions to be free to their full extent. Nothing is lonelier than allowing yourself to cry when there is no one you can trust to comfort you. Martha locked away that risk long ago."

Rebecca wept more freely now. "She really is in pain, isn't she?"

"She is indeed."

"I had no idea that she felt any pain at all. I thought life was so easy for her because she hardly ever got hit. I thought she had it made. And I never dreamed that anyone would think our mother spoiled me." Rebecca shook her head. "All I remember is just trying not to get hit. I can't really remember anything else."

"When all this gets healed, the truth will come clear, and some good things you never noticed before, too, will be restored. Trust me; they will."

*   *   *

Martha rinsed the serving dish, squirted more detergent onto the nylon scrubber, and went at it again, though, if pressed, she would not be able to point out any remaining food. Her movements were rhythmic and followed a pattern of left right, forward back, then around the edges.

Our father hit Rebecca more than Brad and me? Really? How did I never see that? Did Brad really see it as often as he says? Or did he just take her word for it? Why would he make it up? Or did she manipulate him so easily because he felt guilty for leaving?

Her scrubbing slowed. Could she really have missed something that big? No. Impossible. Yet, something in Martha's gut began to tell her that it might be true after all. She couldn't explain it.

The bright kitchen lights shone against night's darkness outside. In her steam-blurred reflection in the window, she saw herself as a child. She stopped scrubbing. A surge of anger arose as she remembered how isolated she had felt. How no one cared about *her*. How ….

A light flashed at the corner of her eye. *Oh, no.* Another migraine? She saw another flicker of light, though this time she realized it was not exactly the same as her migraine lights. The shape wasn't right, and there were … soft colors. She turned to face it more fully. No; nothing there. She scanned the room a moment longer before returning to her work.

She rinsed the dish and balanced it atop the others in the drainer. She took off her gloves and stared at the pyramid of dishes and suddenly felt overwhelmed. Normally she would have dried them right away, but now she felt too exhausted.

She made a decision: tonight, she would go to bed without putting everything away.

She untied her apron and tossed it over the chair back (not on its hook), turned off the light, and left the kitchen. She checked the lock on the front door, and, brushing her hand along the wall, made her way to her bedroom. She peeled off her clothes and tossed them in the general direction of the hamper. She put on her pajamas and climbed into bed. As her head hit the pillow, it occurred to her that she felt thirsty and would have loved a glass of water, but her body would not lift itself to go get one now. She managed to reach the switch at the base of the lamp before drifting off.

For the first time in her life, she fell asleep without brushing her teeth.

*   *   *

Rebecca knelt next to Martha's bed and watched her sister sleep. How could she be related to someone she hardly knew? She watched Martha's face, slack in her stress-and-alcohol-induced sleep—except for an occasional eyebrow twitch—as she slipped into a regular inhale-exhale cycle. Who was this woman? What experiences, what perceptions had she carried with her all these years that Rebecca had no conscious awareness of?

She drew closer to Martha and reached a tentative hand toward her cheek—the cheek of a stranger, yet with a vague resemblance to a memory from long ago. It must have been before Martha felt so unloved. A blurry memory of two little girls, ages three and five, in flannel nightgowns at their grandparents' house, tucked into one bed in the guest room, giggling together, excited about Christmas the next morning. After settling Brad on the couch in the den across the hall, their grandmother had tucked them in and kindly cajoled them, saying that Santa couldn't come until they were really and truly asleep. This thrilled them to greater wakefulness, no matter how hard they tried to calm down. They giggled until their grandmother returned and sat with them, singing gentle songs and stroking their foreheads, gradually melting their resistance, drifting them into slumber with her kind voice.

That was the last Christmas they would spend with their grandmother, their mother's mother. She died the following summer, and Christmases seemed more tension-filled after that. They didn't know why.

Now Rebecca, reflecting on that giggling bedtime with a long-forgotten sister, watched that same sister now and examined her face. Sun damage; more frown lines than any evidence of smiles; faded lipstick; smeared mascara; spiky hair, rather than the soft shoulder-length hair she'd had as a girl. She touched Martha's cheek lightly—so lightly—with the backs of her fingers before pulling away. Nothing happened. Did Martha's heart feel a burden of pain and anger? Was she lonely? Rebecca now realized that the answer to each question was yes.

Remembering how good her grandmother's touch had felt, she tried again, stroking her fingers along Martha's forehead, tentatively at first, then with more confidence, caressing the contour of Martha's head. How long had it been since she had touched her sister, other than when they accidentally brushed against each other at rare family gatherings? She moved her fingers gently along Martha's cheek. Martha continued her regular breathing, apparently unaware of Rebecca's presence.

Rebecca rested her hands on the bed and spoke softly. "Martha, I feel so sad about your pain. It wasn't your fault. Neither one of us is to blame. I understand that now. I hope that someday you can forgive me for taking our mother's attention away from you. I want you to know that *no* one *meant* to hurt you, that it was all a series of terrible human mistakes, and that you did nothing to deserve being ignored. I hope that you can see that there are people who love you."

Martha slept on. Rebecca turned to Lydia. "She doesn't hear any of this, does she?"

"Well, it doesn't appear that way, but you never know. And the important point is that your intention is loving. That will never be wasted. Every intention, every prayer, accomplishes good in some way or another. I know that to be true. Even if it doesn't help Martha, it is already helping you."

They sat quietly for a few minutes while Rebecca pondered these ideas.

After a while, Lydia touched Rebecca's shoulder. "Let's go. We can come back another time."

Rebecca nodded. She stood, hesitated, and then brightened. "But there is one more thing I want to do before I go. I'll be right back!" she said.

Lydia laughed and shook her head, not surprised.

Rebecca vanished and reappeared in Mike and Kate's living room, where Brad slept in the pull-out bed. She watched him sleep, shifting from his side to his back, then to the other side, and on his back again. Rebecca sat on the edge of the bed. She rubbed his shoulder. "Thanks, big brother. You tried super hard. That means the world to me. You're a good brother. No matter how she reacts or doesn't react, you did a loving thing, being that brave and in her face as much as that. You did well. I love you, you dork."

Brad turned on his side and faced Rebecca, though he remained mostly asleep. She gently rubbed his forehead, and he seemed to sink more deeply into his pillow. He didn't move around anymore, and his breathing became more regular.

Rebecca thought of one more thing. "And, hey, you remember Gertrude, my guinea pig? She says hi!"

Brad continued sleeping, but Rebecca thought could see the slightest shift in one eyebrow, and the corners of his mouth turned up for a moment. Rebecca laughed.

"You see?" Lydia stood next to her now. "It works with some people, even if they might never know it."

"I guess I'm not surprised that this seems to help Brad but not Martha," Rebecca replied.

Lydia considered this. "It may not be you who can reach her. Martha is a tough case. Let's go back and talk this over with Eli and the others."

Rebecca gave Lydia a mischievous look and vanished once again.

Lydia chuckled and shook her head. "Of course," she said.

Cuddling Hannah and kissing her face, Rebecca felt newly aware that Reuben had been there not long before. "Was Daddy here?" she asked Hannah.

"Daddy. Bear song!" Hannah giggled.

Rebecca let out a laugh. "I'll be back soon. Good night, my dear one." She kissed Hannah on each cheek, her forehead, her lips, and the top of her head. "I love you, I love you, I love you."

"Night, night," Hannah cooed. "Love, love, love."

*   *   *

A few days later, Kate pulled up in front of Rebecca and Reuben's house, now locked up tight. Martha would meet her there in a half an hour to help, but Kate wanted some time alone before they started to go through Rebecca's things. At the remembrance of the purpose for this day, Kate's heart sank at the recurring realization that Rebecca would not be inside to greet her.

She steeled herself, grabbed her purse, and got out of her car. Heading up the front walk, she noticed the pointed leaves of hyacinths and daffodils that Rebecca had planted a few years earlier, now emerging to greet the early spring. *Can Rebecca see her bulbs now? Her backyard garden? Where is she now? Is she conscious at all? Is she conscious of what's going on here? Or is her world completely different now? When people go ... somewhere else ... do they forget to care about what happens here with those of us left behind?* Kate sniffed in sudden emotion as she found Rebecca's old key, now on her keychain, and fitted it in the lock. With only a bit of jiggling, the lock released to her, and she entered.

The house was dim and cool. Because of the many special times Kate had shared with Rebecca, it still felt welcoming, despite the heavy loss that weighed her down and the solemn strangeness of Rebecca not being here. She entered the living room with the couch facing the stone fireplace. She put her hand to her chest when she saw the couch, remembering times when she and Rebecca had shared long conversations right there. She stepped over to it and sat in her usual spot, to the left of where Rebecca always sat. She put her feet on the pine coffee table and sank into the couch cushions. It wasn't hard to imagine Rebecca right there.

"Oh, Becca!" she lamented softly. "I miss you so much!" She flopped on her side, her head where Rebecca's lap might have been. *You left way too early. I need you here. There is so much left to talk about! What am I going to do, as my girls get older? What am I going to do when you aren't here to tell me how to handle teenagers? How am I going to know what you want me to do when something tough comes up for Hannah?* Kate grabbed a throw pillow and hugged it to her heart. She sank deeper into the couch cushions and wept.

"You'll be okay, Katie." Rebecca whispered to her from her place on the couch. "I know you can do it." Kate shifted and resettled into the cushions. She took a determined gulp of air and quavered as she exhaled. She sniffed, and let the tears continue to fall. Finally, she fell asleep, with Rebecca's hand resting on her forehead.

A knock on the door startled Kate awake. She fumbled up and looked around, still holding the pillow to her chest, disoriented.

"Kate?" She could hear Martha's voice outside the front door.

Oh! Mom. Sort Becca's stuff. Oh no. Okay. Kate dropped the pillow and put her fingers to her temples, and tried to clear her mind before she stood up and staggered to the door.

* * *

Martha stopped at the door to Rebecca's study and scanned the room. A wide desk stood directly across from her, with bookshelves on the right that continued to the next wall. A large window above the desk revealed Rebecca's backyard garden. Along the windowsill and the bookshelves were various rocks (some polished and some in their natural rough state) and shells (not the perfect kind you buy in a gift shop; these must have been found on beach walks). Martha gasped to see, in front of the books on one shelf, a snake skeleton. Recovering from this, she continued her survey. Stacked on the desk up to the windowsill were biology textbooks, a well-worn dictionary, *The Invention Journal of Leonardo da Vinci*, and the complete collection of Gary Larson's *The Far Side*. The blue plaid curtains were open and hooked onto wooden tiebacks. Pausing at a bulletin board to the left of Rebecca's desk, she could see phone messages and slips of paper with scribbles half-covering a calendar. Next to that, a small photo of Albert Einstein with his familiar wild white mane and baggy eyes looking straight into the camera, with his words below: "Anyone who has never made a mistake has never tried anything new."

Martha had never been in here before. In fact, she realized with new clarity, she had never been inside the study of any place where Rebecca had lived. She hadn't seen any of her bedrooms either. Rebecca, though younger, had left home before Martha did. Martha had stayed home until she married Greg. She hadn't felt a need to go to college. She had stayed in town and centered her life around Greg from the beginning. Even after Rebecca came back to town when she married Ted and they had socialized while on the same soccer team, it was usually in a restaurant for burgers or pizza, or barbecuing in a park. Visits in each other's homes over the years had been rare, and they usually involved only the living room or dining room in Ted and Rebecca's apartment. Even back then, Rebecca had always seemed anxious for Martha to leave. And, Martha had to admit, she was more than willing to comply.

Now she stood in what was clearly Rebecca's sanctum. She felt wrong. Unwelcome. Awkward. Intrusive.

But now curious.

And Rebecca was dead. Who else would clean out this house? She couldn't avoid this forever. Jeffrey and Ben would come get Reuben's things, but Rebecca had left the house to Kate. And she couldn't take this on alone. Martha had to help. But how to start, she had no clue. And, though she couldn't explain why, she felt nervous about what she might find.

To fend off her nervousness, she wandered down the hall. Maybe she would go through the linen closet first. Something more neutral.

She opened the linen closet door. But a small sound caught her attention. It sounded like a sniffle, coming from the bedroom where Kate was.

She found Kate sitting on the floor next to a chest of drawers. The large bottom drawer was open and held several flat boxes. On the floor next to the drawer was Rebecca's Girl Scout camp scrapbook. But in Kate's lap sat a box big enough to hold sheets of construction paper of various sizes: some with tempera paint, partially chipped off now; some cut and pasted hearts with a bit of glitter left; some with crayon drawings. Kate hugged one of these drawings to her chest now. She sniffed again and began to sob.

"Kate? Katie? Oh honey, what's wrong?" Martha sat on the floor next to her daughter.

Kate's eyes were red and watery. She lifted the drawing from her chest. "Mom," her voice sounded small. "Mom, look. It's the picture I drew for Becca of her and me having our backyard campfire and sleep out. I was seven." She struggled to pull air into her lungs, and shuddered before letting it go. "Mom, all of these are pictures that I drew for her. See? These are folded 'cause I mailed them to her. Dad helped me address the envelopes. Do you remember? And she kept these," Kate fanned through the pile on her lap. "She kept them all. With all her moving around, she kept my pictures that I gave her, all this time." She wiped some tears away. "And I want to show these to Hannah, but then someday she'll realize that her mom kept my pictures, but *she* can't draw pictures for *her*, and …." Her eyes flooded as she began to sob again in earnest, holding the papers to her heart.

Martha moved closer to hug Kate. But even as she enfolded her daughter in her arms, she felt lonely. What was this relationship between Rebecca and Kate that she had never really tuned into?

Why had she never had that with Rebecca?

*   *   *

Rebecca let herself be carried through the warm iridescent light until she found herself with Lydia in the forest, standing outside the yurt. The sight of Lydia helped her to reorient herself from Kate's and Martha's sadness to being back here. "This is hard for them," she said.

"Yes, it is," Lydia replied gently. She shared the silence with Rebecca for a moment, then gestured toward the yurt. "Let's visit with Mahina for a while." She opened the flap at the entrance and went in. Rebecca followed.

A low, crackling fire awaited them. Rebecca drew in the wood fragrance and relaxed more. The last time she had been here in the yurt, it had been filled with people. Now only Mahina sat cross-legged on the thick carpet facing the fire. When she saw Rebecca and Lydia, she broke into a smile, and gestured toward the fire in welcome. "Come join me, my friends! Would you like some tea?"

Rebecca accepted, and as she and Lydia joined her, they found a tea tray next to them with a large clay pot and three cups. Rebecca poured for everyone, and then took a sip. She tasted orange peel, cinnamon, vanilla, maybe cardamom. Everyone settled into the flavors and aromas for a moment. Rebecca felt a deeper peace than she had felt so far, and it seemed connected to the unexplained familiarity she felt with Mahina. The peace seemed to expand the longer she sat next to her.

Mahina reached for the pot and poured more tea for each of them. Rebecca observed Mahina's hands as she set the pot down and adjusted the lid. Large meaty hands, yet their gentleness and dexterity were evident. She also realized that Mahina was humming a soothing yet joyful tune in her soft alto voice.

Rebecca gaped in recognition. "You!" she said. "I mean … I know you!" Rebecca shook her head and laughed. "I mean, of course I know you! But I recognize you now. In a different way, I mean. When I first met you here in the yurt, I had the feeling I already knew you. And now… are you the one who healed me when I first got here? When all that pain was pulled out of me so gently? I think your humming jogged that memory."

Mahina smiled and nodded, her eyes wet with love.

Rebecca threw herself into Mahina's already open arms and they embraced. She felt so loved, so safe, so at-home. "I feel like I've always known you. Does that make any sense?" Even as she asked, she knew she didn't care whether it made sense or not.

"Makes sense to me," Mahina deepened her hug, and kissed Rebecca's head. They released their embrace and looked into each other's faces, laughing like old friends.

Lydia clapped in delight. "This calls for some cookies!" A plate of her favorites appeared on the table. The three women started in on the cookies and reveled in their flavors.

Finally, Mahina said to Rebecca. "You are concerned about your niece and your sister, and the pain they are feeling."

"Yes," Rebecca replied, hardly surprised that Mahina knew this.

Mahina nodded. "Kate most likely will continue to respond well to your comfort. Even though she has the daunting task of being a mother to your daughter and her own girls, I believe she'll do well. As for your sister …." she paused. "Of course, you know that we all have our own path, our own choices. But there are some things we can do to express love and soften long-established edges. Nevertheless, everyone has the choice to resist any of it. But even if what we try doesn't change anything, when the intention is true, it will never do harm. It could take more than one visit. In fact, it could take many visits. Would you like to try?"

Rebecca smiled at her. "Well, I've heard there's plenty of time."

Mahina's eyes crinkled with amusement. "Yes, I've heard that too. Okay, first, let's get Betty here, and Eli, too. Eli has some special talents to share that might come in handy about now."

A few minutes later, Eli and Betty had joined their circle, and two new teacups had appeared on the tray, along with more cookies.

Eli swigged his tea and set his cup down. He rubbed his wrinkly hands together in anticipation of their new project. "Okay. You've both tried individually," he said to Rebecca and Betty, "and our dear Martha continues to feels too much pain to realize the joys of the life she's been given. It's hard to imagine someone being that sad, and we all want to help her. So now we must work together if we hope to succeed. Our actions carry much more power when we weave our intentions together. You must remember that it's still not guaranteed to work; she always has free choice about whether she will or will not make use of what we are trying to communicate to her. But it seems clear that we all believe we must try. Do you agree?"

*   *   *

"Thanks so much, Isabelle." Martha put the paintbrushes and roller in the sink with water. Now her bedroom walls had a fresh coat of Cilantro Green to cover up the Commodore Blue it had been for so many years with Greg. She needed to mark her territory now that Greg was gone for good. She wanted a fresh start, a new view.

"Are you sure I can't help you finish the cleanup?" Isabelle waited, not yet moving toward the door.

"No, I'm fine. You've helped me a lot. I couldn't have gotten it all done in one day without you. Now I'll be able to sleep with the room already put back to almost normal. Thanks for helping me get the curtains back up."

"If you need some help re-hanging your pictures tomorrow, just let me know."

"I sure will. Thanks."

"Is your family still out of town?" Isabelle asked.

"Yes, they've all gone up to someone's cabin at Lake Tahoe. They wanted to get away."

"You didn't want to go?"

"No, I have too much to do. Maybe next time. Thanks again."

Isabelle hesitated, then put her hand on the doorknob. "Okay, but give me a call if you need to." She stepped outside and clicked the door softly behind her.

Martha stood at the sink and began to squeeze the brush bristles under water, releasing the paint. She could use a vacation. And she loved Tahoe. But not this time. Too many people there she didn't want to see. Kate and Mike and the girls, sure. But then there was Hannah, too, who haunted her with Rebecca's green eyes. And Jeffrey and Ben would be there. She just didn't have the energy to be polite to so many strangers when she felt this exhausted.

She squeezed each brush hard to get out the last of the water, gave them a shake, and propped them on the edge of the sink. She reached for the roller.

And this time Ann would be there, and Ellen, with her friend. Too many people. At least Brad had gone home. *I just can't deal with Brad. What's gotten into him lately? He's a fine one to talk about family. Don't tell me how to live my life, you sanctimonious jerk!*

But now, snapping at Brad in her mind, she found her heart wasn't into it. Maybe she *should* try to work this out. She missed Kate and the girls, even though they lived nearby. She couldn't keep herself busy enough to hide the fact that she missed babysitting Naomi and Fiona lately. She couldn't stop doing that just to avoid Hannah. That would make *her* miserable. It wasn't Hannah's fault that she looked like Rebecca. Maybe she should have gone this weekend.

No. She couldn't deal with all those people. No.

She turned the water on full force and let it run over the roller as she squeezed and turned it, over and over, letting the green paint run out, out, out, and yet more kept coming. *Brad and all his psychobabble. No one will just leave well enough alone.* Martha squeezed and turned, squeezed and turned. *How much paint can one roller absorb?* Cloudy green water kept pouring out.

*　　　　*　　　　*

Melting snowdrifts surrounded the rented Tahoe cabin. Inside, Hannah sank into sleep in Kate's lap. Ellen and her friend, Gretchen, sat at a nearby table with Ann, playing scrabble. Brutus, the black Lab, sprawled on the floor between Ellen and the hearth, monitoring comings and goings with occasional eyebrow shifts.

"Boy, Jeffrey and Ben have been in there a long time," Mike said, referring to them taking charge of story time with Fiona and Naomi in the bedroom down the hall. He added a log to the fire and watched it while rubbing Brutus's ears.

"The girls are getting really good at manipulating them into extra stories," Kate laughed.

Ann, waiting for Ellen to decide what word to arrange on the board, went to the coffee table to refill her wine glass. She turned to Kate, "So, our little one is doing well?"

"Ann, she's a marvel. I mean, my girls were both pretty content when they were this young, but Hannah is astounding. She is happy all the time, and I swear, she looks at me like she has a fun joke to tell me, but she just can't figure out how to say it."

"Oh, I'm glad. That sure makes this whole transition easier. Rebecca and Reuben would be proud of her."

"Something else we didn't expect is that she's always more than willing to go to bed every night. Our girls were such night owls at this age. We read stories to her and sing a few songs, then, after I've turned out the light and left the room, a little while later, I hear her in there, singing to herself. And it's not necessarily a song we just sang. It's funny. She just seems to know how to entertain herself before she falls asleep."

"Hm. Interesting," Ann mused.

Rebecca and Reuben shimmered into the room. Brutus lifted his head immediately, looked straight at them, and clambered to his feet. He wagged his tail, sneezed, snorted, and danced a bit. Then Jeffrey came around the corner.

"Oh. Brutus must have heard you coming," Mike said. "How are the girls doing?"

"They're asleep now. And so is Ben," Jeffrey grinned. "I guess they wore him out."

Brutus kept dancing until Rebecca greeted him with kisses on his nose, which made him sneeze. Then he calmed down, though his tail kept wagging.

"I guess he's getting attached to you," Ellen said to Jeffrey.

Jeffrey gave Brutus a puzzled look before he grabbed a beer and sat next to Mike on the couch. Brutus didn't follow him, but kept focusing on the center of the room, presumably happy to see everyone gathered at the cabin.

*   *   *

Martha finished the last bit of her tortellini dinner and poured herself another glass of zinfandel. On the TV, Columbo returned for the umpteenth time with "just one more question" for the man he, of course, already knew was the murderer. Martha had immersed herself in these reruns lately. It felt good to think about someone else's problems.

As the credits rolled on the second rerun of the night,

Martha clicked off the TV and drained the last of the wine from her glass. She'd been drinking more than usual lately, but hey, she had worked hard all day, painting. She'd earned it. And adjusting to divorce was hard work.

She tossed the microwave packages into the trash, put her fork and glass in the dishwasher, and meandered to bed. The paint was probably dry enough now, but she'd wait until tomorrow to hang her pictures again. She collapsed into bed and fell asleep with no further thoughts.

*   *   *

Eli, Betty, and Rebecca entered Martha's bedroom. Eli watched her sleep for a few minutes. Rebecca watched his face as he did so. He seemed to be examining Martha—not superficially, but intuitively, seeking insights, or a strategy, or, Rebecca wasn't quite sure what.

Finally, he turned to Betty and Rebecca. "Okay," he said, nodding. "I think you've both talked to her enough. She needs some action—some imagery. And ...." Here he gestured back and forth between Rebecca and her mother. "We've got some good parallel action going on here. Three cords and all that." He smiled, apparently happy with his train of thought. "You both know that we're not really supposed to move or pick up anyone, but on an energetic level, the *idea* of moving can happen quite easily. Betty, what do you love most about watching Rebecca with Hannah?"

"Oh, I love the way she rocks her and sings to her. I love that when she hugs her, Hannah seems to soak in the love and it is obvious how happy it makes her."

"Exactly," Eli nodded enthusiastically. "And?"

"And this is what I want to do for Martha," Betty said, her voice wobbling. "I've tried before—as you know—over and over, and there's been no effect. I need help," she gulped and stopped talking.

Eli gently moved his hands above Betty's heart until her breathing steadied. She took another long breath and let it out easily, then smiled. "It will be okay," she said. Rebecca put an arm around her and kept it there, amazed that this was now a comfortable thing to do. Betty leaned into the hug. Both women looked at each other, silently acknowledging their new mutual appreciation before they gave each other one more squeeze and turned back to Eli.

Eli watched them for a minute. "Okay," he said. "Martha's a tough case, so we are going to band together here. And your instinct to sing to her will be especially helpful. Sung words are often integrated more easily than spoken words." Eli stepped over to Martha, who was sleeping deeply. He gently moved his hands over her. Rebecca noticed the same tiny flashes of multicolored light that she thought she'd seen earlier in his eyes, now emanating from his fingers. Those light shimmers remained above Martha even when he turned to Rebecca and moved his hands over her head and then did the same over Betty. The multicolored light remained over them as well. It wasn't bright; they might not have noticed it if they hadn't seen it first appear; but they felt it, as well, a soft subtle vibration of nurturing and calm energy.

"We are adding threads to Martha's dream loom," Eli explained to them solemnly, although his lavender eyes still sparkled with their usual joy. "It's temporary, and we don't use it often, but I think it's worth a try here."

Rebecca nodded, and though she didn't exactly understand what Eli meant, she felt eager to proceed.

"Now. Rebecca, don't try to predict what the plan is here. Answer me this: what—in your gut—do you most want to do right now?"

Rebecca immediately knew, though she hadn't a moment ago. "I want to go see Hannah."

"Go."

"Really?" Rebecca was surprised at this. Weren't they supposed to be focusing on Martha?

"Trust your gut," Eli said. "Go."

Hannah's breathing was soft and steady as she neared sleep. But she awakened fully when she saw Rebecca. She looked just above her head at the colorful shimmer. "Ooh, pretty!" she exclaimed.

Rebecca laughed. "Hello, sweet one," she said, and snuggled next to her daughter. Then, just a few yards beyond the bed, she saw her mother through a gauzy iridescence, standing next to Martha but watching Rebecca, smiling. Surprised—but not surprised—that they could see each other though the houses were miles apart, Rebecca turned to Hannah. "Which song would you like tonight?" she asked.

"'Goodnight, My Dear One!'" Hannah demanded eagerly.

"Okay." Rebecca and Hannah had it memorized by now. She put her arms around Hannah and rocked her to the gentle tune.

> Goodnight my dear one, your quilt awaits
> To wrap you warm, and bless your dreams
> Pillows tenderly cradle you
> Sink soft in your bed, safe and loved
>
> Stars beckon you to join their dance
> In the Milky Way sky above
> Enchanted in celestial ballet
> They smile on you, beautiful child
>
> Now with you here, the world is kinder
> My heart overflows with love for you
> Your light shines bright upon us all
> My life's treasure, my greatest joy
>
> My love surrounds you, near and far
> Love surrounds you, now and always
> When you awake and venture forth
> My love will surround you still

Betty watched for a moment, and found herself eager to sing the song again that she had sung so many times before, unheard. But more than that, now she knew that it was the music itself and the energy behind it, more than the words, that would carry her intention. She climbed onto the bed next to Martha, who lay asleep on her side, facing away from her mother. Betty combed her fingers through Martha's hair and kissed her head. She sang the verses slowly so that Martha would absorb every word. And she felt the tune carry her as she held her daughter and gently rocked her to the rhythm of the lullaby.

> Goodnight my dear one, your quilt awaits
> To wrap you warm, and bless your dreams
> Pillows tenderly cradle you
> Sink soft in your bed, safe and loved
>
> Stars beckon you to join their dance
> In the Milky Way sky above
> Enchanted in celestial ballet
> They smile on you, beautiful child

Tears began to trickle from Martha's eyes, and she hiccupped, though Betty knew that her daughter was still asleep. She caressed Martha's head and kissed her, then resumed singing.

> Now with you here, the world is kinder
> My heart overflows with love for you
> Your light shines bright upon us all
> My life's treasure, my greatest joy
>
> My love surrounds you, near and far

Love surrounds you, now and always
When you awake and venture forth
My love will surround you still

By the time Betty finished all of the verses, Martha had stopped crying. She rolled onto her back, and, with a long exhale, seemed to fall into a deeper sleep. Betty touched Martha's heart. "I love you, Martha." She placed her hand on her daughter's heart and repeated, "I love you, I love you, I love you."

* * *

Martha awoke. The light coming through her window seemed high in the sky. What time was it? She never slept this late. She rubbed the corners of her eyes. They were a bit crusty, as though they had been watering a lot in her sleep, though she couldn't imagine why. Sitting up, she felt light-headed. How much did she drink last night? She didn't feel headachy, though, the way she did some mornings lately, after overdoing it. In fact, her head felt good, just different. Maybe it was the fresh-paint fumes that made her feel funny.

She climbed out of bed and walked over to the window. She felt lighter on her feet, not shuffling the way she usually did in the mornings. She pulled the curtain aside. In her window box, the tulips, which Isabelle had given her when Rebecca died, were opening. Pinks, whites, reds. They really were beautiful, now that she stopped to look. She reached out and gently

238

traced a finger along the petals, first one bloom, then another.

She sniffled and her vision blurred. What? How could she feel emotion for flowers? But how could she not? She felt confused for a moment, but couldn't resist immersing herself in the feelings that came with the sight of these beautiful flowers. She touched her face and realized that it was wet with new tears.

*   *   *

The next night, Eli, Rebecca, and Betty met again in Martha's room.

Eli stood in front of Betty and said, "This time, you do it." He waited, watching her.

"Excuse me?" Betty looked at him quizzically.

"Ah, my dear Betty," Eli smiled at her with affection. "You are more powerful than you realize. You know what to do. Have faith in yourself." He put both hands on her head. Betty's eyebrows shot up as the multi-colored light entered her head and burst forth from her palms.

Eli gave them both an impish grin and vanished.

Betty and Rebecca gaped at one another.

"Well," Betty said, shrugging. "Here goes." She walked over to Martha, and gently moved her hands over her. Rebecca could see the same tiny flashes of light come out of Betty's hands that she had seen from Eli's the night before. Betty watched as the colorful light shimmers remained above Martha. Then she turned and moved her hands over Rebecca, then over herself.

Awestruck, they could see the colorful starry lights around each other.

"Way to go, Mom!" Rebecca blurted.

The women both laughed and took their places, Betty next to Martha, Rebecca with Hannah, and sang to their daughters.

*   *   *

The next morning, after pondering over her coffee, Martha impulsively grabbed the phone and dialed. She left a message, and hung up.

What had possessed her to do *that*?

*   *   *

It was well past midnight when Brad got home from the birthday party his friends had thrown for him right after work. Even though it was late, he wasn't a bit tired. He checked his voicemail.

"Brad? It's Martha. I just wanted to wish you a happy birthday. I hope you've been having a good day. Bye."

Whoa. Brad hadn't talked with Martha since that night at her house after the ash-scattering ceremony. She hadn't let him come back the next morning before he caught his flight. He wasn't sure if she would ever speak to him again.

She hasn't called me on my birthday since … well, ever.

What's going on?

*   *   *

When Betty and Rebecca met in Martha's room the next night, Eli gestured between the two women, and nodded, as if they should understand by now what he intended. Through the gauzy colored light that bridged the two bedrooms together, they saw a sycamore tree with a rope swing. Eli walked toward this now, and seated himself on it. He smiled and waved at them, then turned his attention to swinging as high as he could under the starry sky.

The two women were a bit stunned for a moment. But then Betty took a breath and adjusted her stance. She put both of her hands on Rebecca's head, and said, "Now you."

A soft vibration that felt both nurturing and invigorating moved through Rebecca's brain and down her arms, until she could see colors shooting out of her palms. As much as this energy kept leaving her palms, it never subsided within her. Open-mouthed, she exchanged smiles with Betty as she placed her hands on her mother's head, then on Martha's. The flow of colored light never diminished, and, in fact, Rebecca wondered if it might have even increased. She felt a joyful calm strength, greater than what she had experienced so far.

Hannah smiled sleepily at Rebecca when she appeared, and snuggled deeper into her bed to listen to her mother's voice. And the end of the song, both women touched their daughters' hearts and once again told them, "I love you, I love you, I love you," before returning to the yurt, where Mahina met them.

"All right," she said. "Now we let your work take effect. Go rest. Go play."

*   *   *

"Thanks for coming over, Mom." Kate finished cutting up the mushrooms and began to chop onions. "I don't think I could get this done by myself with the girls home today."

"Happy to help. So, what did Mike request for his birthday dinner?" Martha asked.

"Beef stroganoff over spaghetti squash."

Martha raised her eyebrows. "Well, that's different," she said.

Kate smiled. "By the way, when the cake is ready to frost, the girls asked if they could help. I'm wondering if you could distract Hannah while they do that with me. She doesn't exactly have the coordination for it yet, and I'm just picturing a mess that I don't want to deal with."

Martha hesitated. So far, she'd been pretty good at avoiding Hannah.

"Mom, *please.*" Kate didn't want to get into it with Martha today.

Naomi rushed into the room. "Grammy, come see what we're making!"

"On my way, dear," Martha said. She followed Naomi toward the family room, but stopped in the doorway to look back at Kate.

"Okay. I'll do it," she said bravely. She even attempted a smile.

Warm spicy aromas of the freshly baked carrot cake permeated the house. It was ready to frost.

Kate didn't like the kids to watch much TV, but she was desperate. "Hannah! Would you like to watch *Bunny Ballet*?" She set up the video, and Hannah plunked herself onto the beanbag chair, instantly engrossed, not noticing her sisters leave the room with Kate.

Martha sat quietly on the couch behind Hannah with her cup of coffee. At least she didn't have to entertain her. That made it easier. She sipped her coffee and settled into the cushions. The video actually did have some nice artwork, nice animation. She wasn't really in the mood to take on a four-year-old and a six-year-old frosting a cake anyway. And this was working out well, Hannah being mesmerized with the dancing bunnies and all.

Now it was time for the little girl bunny to brush her teeth and put on her jammies. The mommy bunny tucked her into bed. "Goodnight, my little bunny," the mommy bunny said.

Hannah watched the bunnies on TV. "Good night, my dear one," she said softly.

Martha gasped and her heart raced. "What?" she blurted in a much shriller voice than she had intended. "What did you say?" She gawked at Hannah in confusion. Maybe she had heard wrong. Maybe that same dream that she had had the last several nights lingered in her mind. Wait. *What dream?* She hadn't thought about a dream until now.

Hannah turned and smiled shyly at Martha. "Good night, my dear one."

Martha put her hand to her chest. Her mind swirled with gradual recognition. To her consternation, tears began to stream down her face.

Hannah climbed out of the beanbag and toddled over to Martha on the couch. "Awww, honey bunny," she said. She climbed up onto the couch, and before Martha knew it, Hannah was in her lap, her face up close. She put her hand on Martha's heart and patted it softly three times. "Love, love, love," she said right into Martha's wet face.

Martha felt a whirlwind in her mind and heart. She didn't understand it, but she found herself looking back at Hannah, whose sincere green eyes—Rebecca's eyes—searched hers with a smiling curiosity. How could this be happening? Her tears would not stop. But she felt something inside her release and the whirlwind slowed. Hannah now grasped Martha's shoulders and squeezed them in little massaging motions, repeating, "Awww, honey bunny." And before Martha could stop herself, she wrapped her arms around Hannah and kissed her cheek. She couldn't stop crying as she rocked her sister's little girl.

*   *   *

Rebecca and Betty watched Martha and Hannah still hugging on the couch. Rebecca brushed tears from her cheeks reflexively, though she didn't really care that they kept falling down her face. Betty, ignoring her own tears, gave Rebecca a joyous squeeze. Then they relaxed into each other and shared relieved laughter. "Thank you!" they both whispered, almost simultaneously. With one arm still around each other, they turned to Eli.

"It's a miracle, isn't it?" Betty said.

Eli threw open his scrawny arms and laughed. "Another miracle!" He hugged them both enthusiastically, and faded away with a luminescent shimmer.

After a reflective moment, Betty loosened her embrace, and said decisively, "Now. We need a break. Why don't you find Reuben and go play? Play with the dogs, or eat some ice cream, or something. The ice is broken. Let them work things out on their own for a while."

*   *   *

Two Years Later

Martha sat at her kitchen table with Hannah. At four and a half, Hannah had every Friday off from preschool. Her favorite choice was to spend those Fridays with Martha. And for Martha, Friday was now her favorite day of the week.

After a short knock, Isabelle let herself in. "Am I too late for the tea party?"

"No, no; in fact, we haven't quite started yet," Martha scooted over happily, making room for Isabelle. "We got immersed in our finger painting and lost track of time." Hannah held up her smeary yellow-blue-green hands and wiggled them at Isabelle, baring all her teeth while she was at it. Little blobs of paint lobbed onto the black-and-white checkered floor, which by now had quite a few stains from art projects past.

When the tea party was just getting into full swing, they heard another knock on the door.

"Come in!" the three yelled with abandon.

The door opened cautiously. "Hello?" Ellen stepped into the kitchen.

"Come on in," Martha said in a hearty voice.

Ellen came in, stepping around the paint spatters and crumpled paper towels strewn on the floor. "Thanks for the invitation," she said. I haven't been to a tea party in ages. I'm sorry I'm late."

"Not a problem at all, Ellen; Martha assured her. "We're so happy you could come. In fact, I was just telling Hannah how you and Rebecca used to finger paint at your house when you two were her age. We'd love to hear about that."

"I'd be happy to tell some Rebecca stories," Ellen said.

"You want some tea?" Hannah asked.

"Oh, yes, my dear, I'd love some tea," Ellen said in her best fancy tea party voice. Martha held out a cup to Hannah, who got onto her knees in her chair and poured, slopping tea onto the table. Martha smiled and handed the too-full cup to Ellen, slopping plenty of tea herself. Ellen took a seat and joined the party.

*   *   *

Rebecca and Reuben sat on Martha's kitchen counter and hugged closer.

"You think we'll be able to visit Hannah and the boys indefinitely?" he asked.

"I know we will," she said. "But ... I never thought I'd say this, but now that we've seen how well Hannah is doing with Mike and Kate, and the girls, and your boys, and now even Martha, it feels like she's in the loving capable hands we've always wanted for her. It feels easy to relax now. And I love that Ellen is here too."

"Yes. All is well," he beamed at her.

She leaned into him, feeling satisfied.

He sat up straighter. "Let's go dancing," he said.

"Now you're talking! Where do you want to go?"

"I was thinking of the place you always wanted to see before we wound up here," he said. "Do you remember?"

A grin spread across her face. "Aurora borealis!"

He extended his hand to hers, and they jumped off the counter. "Let's go!

ACKNOWLEDGEMENTS

Writing this story was an absolute joy, and there are many who helped to make it so.

Thank you to Kathryn Reiss, for her enthusiasm and expert guidance during the early gestation of this story.

To Jamie Harms, who read and re-read countless versions. She became emotionally involved with my characters, gave constructive feedback, and freely shared her medical knowledge, sensibilities and concerns.

To Melissa Nilsen, for her creative spirit and first-hand advice about what it feels like to be in labor, as well as countless re-reads and valuable feedback.

To Mr. Sigg, my 11th grade English and Creative Writing teacher, who unrelentingly urged us to be truthful, even in fiction.

To Mrs. Ingenthron, my 7th grade English teacher, who wrote at the top of every one of my stories, "have you considered becoming a writer?" I have, I am, and I thank you.

And finally, to my husband, Tim Calvert, who, along with his undying support of my writing, always gives honest feedback, and in many instances, saved Reuben's self-respect when he let me know that "a guy would never say it that way." Reuben thanks you, and so do I.

ABOUT THE AUTHOR

Photo by Lyn Whiting

Christie Monson's idea of heaven includes abundant gardens, gourmet meals, and animals who can finally tell you what they think. A lifelong reader and writer, she loves characters who are under-represented, truth seekers, and fond of hilarity. She and her husband, along with their nutty dog, divide their time between the Central California coast and the Sierra foothills. This is her first novel.

She can be reached at ChristieMonson.com.

CPSIA information can be obtained
at www.ICGtesting.com
Printed in the USA
FSHW010635011020
74274FS